HUNTING FOR LOVE

KACI LANE

AUTHOR NOTE

Hunting for Love is the first book in the Bama Boys Sweet RomCom Series. I also wrote a companion book to the series, *Christmas in Dixie*, which is set in Apple Cart County and includes many of the same characters.

If you want to keep up with all my books and get updates about opportunities to receive Advanced Reader Copies as well as backstories on my content, join my newsletter.

Happy reading!

Kaci :)

HUNTING FOR LOVE

CHAPTER ONE

Bianca

I'm the man. Uh, I mean the woman. Whatever. I just bagged another high-profile client. Dad will be thrilled.

My stilettos click across the marble floor leading to his office. If it weren't for having to prove my professionalism to all the mad men in this place, I'd be skipping right now. That, and the fact that my pencil skirt won't allow for it.

I stop in front of his door and smooth my blond hair before knocking. I suck in a breath and impatiently wait for the boss-king to lower his scepter and let me enter. Favorite daughter aside, he still makes me play by protocol.

His gruff voice echoes from the other side. "Come in."

I turn the brass knob and push the door like a linebacker shoving through the offensive line. I swear, his door weighs more than me. Probably to keep people from barging in unannounced. "Dad?"

His thick eyebrows arch like two caterpillars stretching.

I'd tried taking him to my brow girl, but he'd insisted only women and millennial hipsters waste money on such nonsense. And I can't argue with that.

"Come in, Bianca."

I cross the slick floor and sit on the sofa facing his desk. I sink into the puffy leather and relax my shoulders. The corners of my mouth tug upward as I announce my win with pride. "Maker's Makeup is a now a client."

Dad widens his eyes, stretching the caterpillars into a downward dog position. "Very good. I have another prospective client I'd like you to meet."

I wiggle with anticipation. While I enjoy helping clients manage their money, my favorite part is the travel. Maybe he would send me someplace tropical this time.

Dad puts on his reading glasses. I swallow back a giggle. I'd offered to buy him a new pair, but he prefers the pair he's had for years. The pair that makes him look like Benjamin Franklin. He fumbles through a stack of folders on the edge of his desk and pulls one in front of him.

"There's a sporting goods chain out West doing so well, they want to expand to our side of the country."

"Atlanta?"

"Georgia and other states."

I squint and lean forward to try to sneak a peek at the folder's contents. Georgia, Tennessee. And that's all I get before he picks up the folder and swivels his chair to the side.

"Let's see here." He adjusts his Revolutionary-era viewfinders. Please be Florida. I could use some heat after a week in New York.

"Georgia, Tennessee, Mississippi, and Alabama."

My face drops. "So, am I going to their main branch?" Please let it be some nice-sized city.

Dad removes his glasses and clears his throat. "No,

they're coming this way to scout out locations, so I've arranged for you to meet with them in Alabama."

Acid boils through my stomach. Alabama?

Aside from passing through the state, I'd been there exactly twice in my life. Once with my sorority sisters for a football game, then a year ago when we were in negotiations with a barbecue company in Birmingham. Alabama had beaten Georgia State, and the barbecue company had said they couldn't trust a vegetarian to run their funds. The only good that came out of that was me branching out into eating chicken. You know, for the business, of course.

"Before you ask, it's not Birmingham."

I exhale a breath I hadn't realized I was holding. My stomach suddenly feels ten pounds lighter. Maybe I could skip barre class tonight.

"It's in . . ." Dad props the Ben Franks back onto the bridge of his nose. "Apple Cart."

I laugh so hard I snort. "Apple Cart? Are you kidding me?" I meet his eyes. The caterpillars say he wasn't kidding. My laugh lines dissolve to nothing. "That's the name of the town?"

He nods. "There's a large orchard there or something to that effect."

"And they want to build a sporting goods store there?"

"Not necessarily, but it's a good central location for all the places they want to scout."

I squish back into the couch and let out a puff of air. "Wait, so they found the central location between the spots where they actually want to go and decided to meet there? Despite the place being best known for apples?" Nothing about this makes sense. No wonder these people need us.

"It is central, but it also has a new hunting lodge. The men booked it so they could hunt between meetings."

Oh great. "A hunting lodge?"

"Don't worry. You won't have to hunt."

Well, that's reassuring. A nervous laugh squeaks from my drying throat. I reach for Dad's coffee mug and turn it up like a shot of whiskey. Ugh. I wince at the black, bitter liquid. I'd have been better off shooting whiskey.

"Are you okay?" He gives me his skeptical stare.

I set the mug back on his desk and nod, while trying to lick the dregs of pure coffee beans off my teeth. "You'd make me stay at a lodge in a place called Apple Pie?"

"Apple Cart."

I wave a manicured hand his way. "Whatever. Dad, I've never gone to camp before."

He shrugged his shoulders. "Think of it as an adventure."

Had he lost his mind? Why couldn't they just come to Atlanta? These rednecks could stop and shoot things on their way home.

"Why don't you meet with them, Dad? At least you've been quail hunting before."

He rocks back in his chair and steeples his fingers. Uh oh. He's about to give me the speech. "Bianca, do you want to run this company someday?" And there it is.

"More than anything." I mean that with all my heart. From the time I was a little girl coming to my daddy's office, to getting a degree in finance and then my MBA. And I'd worked my tushy off as an employee, trying to prove myself as a natural dealmaker.

He leans across the desk and meets my eyes. The caterpillars have straightened into corpse pose, meaning he is dead serious. "Then you need to learn that there's more business to be made than just makeup, spas, and fashion."

I allow the couch to swallow my shoulders, then lower my gaze. My eyes blur as I stare at the subtle dot pattern in my tweed skirt. Dad made a valid point. Up until now, I'd focused on the projects that appealed to me, with the exception of the barbecue company. Of course, he'd suggested I spearhead that one. Wait a minute . . .

"Is that why you sent me to Birmingham last year?"

The corner of his mouth cocks into a mischievous smile.

I tilt my head. "Dad. Why?" How could he smile, knowing what I'd endured?

"Because, daughter, when you're in this office, you're my employee first. You have to learn how to connect with all types of people, whether they like tofu and handbags or meat and handguns."

A chill shoots down my spine. I'd never touched an actual gun. The few Dad owned stayed locked in a safe at my childhood home. And now he wanted me to close a deal with men who sold guns for a living? How was that supposed to work?

"Bianca, you can do this."

I nod reluctantly. I could do this. I had to do this. But . . . "One question."

"What's that?"

"This lodge . . ." The word "lodge" came out like a swear word, causing me to cringe. "Is it like in *The Parent Trap*?" I sit up straight. "I mean, will I be sleeping in a wooden shack and showering in a stall that shows my feet?"

He wipes a hand across his wrinkled forehead and chuckles. "You'll have your own room and bathroom."

I close my eyes. The knot in my stomach loosens. This conversation has been a killer ab workout.

"You can do this. And if you plan to take over this company when I retire, you'll have to."

That was all I needed to hear. I had to make this work. "So when do I leave?"

"Tomorrow morning. Your flight for Birmingham leaves at five. You can get a car to take you from there."

Birmingham. My mind flashed back to the last time I'd

landed in that gloomy city of steel and pig butts. It was nothing more than a wannabe Atlanta. Not that Apple Cart sounded any more appealing. But it was doubtful a town called Apple Cart had made any efforts to try and best my beloved Hotlanta.

"Did you hear me?"

I shake my head to focus, then turn my eyes to dad's. "Yes."

He could always could sense when I got lost in my thoughts. Just like I could sense when he was testing me.

But why did all his tests have to happen in Alabama?

I yawn for the forty-seventh time while waiting in line at the airport Starbucks. Apparently, everyone else up at this ungodly hour also needs coffee to function. Flights before seven should be outlawed. If the pilot is half as sleepy as me, we're in for trouble.

I step up to the counter at last. "Venti Blonde vanilla latte, non-fat milk, no foam." I hand the barista my credit card and adjust my leopard-print pencil skirt. Packing for this trip had posed quite the challenge. I'd wanted to mesh with the wilderness theme of the lodge and still retain my professional appearance.

"Thanks." I retrieve my card and shift toward the small crowd waiting on their drinks.

"Venti Blonde vanilla latte for Bianca."

Ah. I smile as I lift the cup from the counter and walk toward the terminal. I find a seat in the front row by the gate. I turn the drink in my hand, then narrow my eyes. The scribbling of my name looks at lot like "Biatch." I shrug. It's not like I haven't been called that before. I take a sip of the latte, pausing to relish the warm vanilla liquid as it trickles down my throat. Delicious. Every drop worth being "Biatch."

I pull out a folder from my carryon. Time for a crash course on the prospective client, as well as the lodge.

"Gamer's Paradise Lodge." I giggle. Was this a hunting lodge or a redneck spoof song? I sigh and type the name into my phone. Sure enough, Google asked if I meant to search for "Gangsta's Paradise." I scroll past all the song-related results until I see Gamer's Paradise Lodge.

I click on the website. Geez Louise. How many photos of deer and turkey would I have to scroll past to get to something good? Finally, an image without wildlife. Oh, wait. A bunch more photos of open fields. A waste of space, if you ask me. Then, like a diamond in the rough, a gorgeous log mansion pops up.

I straighten in my seat and zoom in on the lodge. No church camp cabin here. This house could hold its own at any upscale ski resort. I continue to the interior shots. High-end wood furnishings and burgundy leather couches, complete with animal skin rugs and antler chandeliers. Quite the pleasant surprise, given its surroundings.

"Now boarding our platinum members . . ." A friendly female voice leaks from the overhead speakers.

I perk up at the announcement. I chuck my phone in my purse and down the last of my coffee, shuddering at the sudden surge of heat hitting my throat. Then, I grab my carryon and head for the terminal gate.

Buildings shrink and land expands the higher the plane climbs. I recline my head and search the app on my phone for a car to pick me up. I start checking off exclusions. No men, no recent tickets, no teenagers, no smokers. One total match for the time I need. I guess we have a winner. I book the driver just as the pilot announces the upcoming landing.

We descend on an expanse of concrete between trees and houses. Not the high-rise landscapes of Atlanta. But Birmingham has at least one quality Atlanta doesn't. An easy-to-maneuver airport. After deplaning, I retrieve my bags in record time without once having to elbow through a sea of people.

I step outside and squint against the sun. I pull my Coach sunglasses over my eyes, then check my phone for the driver's name and car description.

Miles of asphalt and cars cloud my view. Then, I spot it —a white Honda with a dented door and a missing front hubcap. The car has seen better days. I suck in a breath and remind myself that I chose it for the driver's profile and ratings. A woman around my age gets out of the driver's side when I come closer.

"I'm Angie." She extends a slim hand, and I shake it.

"Bianca. Thanks for the last-minute ride."

"No problem."

I shove my bag in the backseat and climb in beside it. A stack of notebooks litters the floorboard. I shift my feet to avoid stepping on them. Once I settle in, my head hits something stuffy. I turn to find a duffle bag shoved behind my seat.

"Sorry for the mess." Angie frowns in the rearview mirror.

"It's okay." I force a smile. It's not *that* okay. Messy and unprofessional, yes. But still better than riding with a male chauvinistic smoker or some kid fresh off getting their license.

"So, Apple Cart, is it?"

"Yes."

I use the long drive to study the prospective client file,

glancing out the window now and again. The storefronts grow fewer and farther between until farms and houses replace them completely. Apple Cart, Alabama. So that's where the phrase "off the beaten path" originated.

We ride past an orchard with more trees than a Christmas tree lot. A stretch of land this long would be prime real estate in downtown Atlanta. But in a place called Apple Cart, they probably want to keep it in apples. A few miles later, the town's welcome sign comes into view. Angie stops the car at a red light, then turns away from downtown. My chest sinks as we ride farther from actual town, passing everything from cotton fields to long metal buildings that smell like poop.

At last, I see a sign for Gamer's Paradise. Angie starts down a dirt drive. Dust flies up beside my window. I smirk. Better Angie's old beater than my Mercedes. After a few yards, Angie suddenly stops.

I lean forward. "What is it?"

She stomps the gas. The car revs but doesn't move. She hits the gas again, and rocks sling up. A few beat against the windows, quickening my heartbeat. Angie's eyes widen. Not good.

"Uh, I don't think that's helping. Maybe you should stop."

She removes her hands from the wheel. I roll down my window and crane my neck over the door to survey the damage. Mud covers at least half of the back tire. Yep. We are stuck. I slump back in my seat, hitting my head again on the duffle bag. I groan. "Welcome to Apple Cart, Bianca."

Jack

I pour another bucket of corn into the feeder, then check the varmint guard. Crazy raccoons. How I'd love to add them to the endangered species list. But hunting rogue coons won't fix the root of the problem.

As I reach into my toolbox for a screwdriver, my phone buzzes. Unknown number. I hesitate a split second, then tap the screen to answer. One downfall to using my personal number for business. I can't afford to miss something important.

"Jack. Gamer's Paradise."

A strident female voice blasts my ear. I wince and hold the phone a few inches away.

"Calm down, ma'am." More hysterics. I roll my eyes and wait for her to run out of breath. "Yes, ma'am. Don't panic. I'll be there as soon as I can."

After a less than appreciative response, I hang up the phone and stuff it in the front pocket of my Carhartt over-alls. I climb into my Dodge pickup and head for the entrance. I make it almost to the end of the drive before I pull up to an older Honda. The back tires are sunk low into fresh mud.

I remove my cap and run a hand through my hair. Most people had sense not to drive through mud in a car like that. I really should resurface that road with a new load of gravel, but still. Too bad my money is tied up in other things. Liking paying the mortgage.

I settle my cap back onto my head and hop out of the truck. "Hey, I'm Jack."

A tall, skinny blond standing beside the front of the car looks up from her phone and scowls. The most interesting green eyes glare a hole through me. "Finally."

This is without a doubt the woman who made me hard

of hearing a few minutes ago. I stare back at her, then allow myself to take in her high cheekbones and long legs. I land on her eyes again. Those majestic green marbles shoot daggers at me.

I swallow and drop my gaze. Too bad the attitude doesn't match the outside packaging. I lick my lips and search for something to say. "Is this your car?"

She laughs, a combination between a cheerleader and Cruella De Vil. Disturbing, yet original. "No, I got a ride-share." She looks back at her phone.

I march through the mud to the other side and knock on the window to settle this with the driver. Blondie can play on her phone, for all I care. A woman behind the wheel jumps, then rolls down the window.

Wow. The last time two hot women came to the lodge was when the local Junior League brought me a house-warming gift. Unfortunately, I'd found the lasagna and sweet potato casserole way more appealing than either of them.

"Hi, I'm Angie."

"Hey, Angie, I'm Jack. I'm gonna hook my truck to the front of your car and pull you out. Okay?"

The brunette nods. "Can I get her bags first?" She seems sweet. Why is it always the blonds who cause trouble?

"I can get them. Where are they?"

Angie points to two large bags and a smaller one in the backseat. Hard to miss as the bigger ones are bright blue with spots, like exotic animal markings. Ugliest things I've seen. And I've seen a lot of ugly in my twenty-seven years.

I open the back door and snatch the bags by the handles, then move them to the bed of my truck.

Blondie unglues her eyes from the phone and narrows them at me. "Careful with those! My purse is Italian leather."

I ignore her and shut the car door. I go around to the front and search for a secure place to hook the winch, finding one that's a decent enough spot. I pull the winch from my truck and secure it tightly. Then, I walk back to Angie's window.

"Angie, crank your car. I'll start pulling, and when you feel it start to move, slowly press the gas."

She nods again, her face looking a little panicked.

"It's going to be okay."

She halfway smiles, her face relaxing a little.

Blondie stays off to the side, scrolling through her phone.

I walk closer to her. "Uh, ma'am?" She pays me zero attention. I raise my voice. "Ma'am!"

She flinches and raises her head.

"I need you to back up a couple of yards. Possibly more."

She props a hand on her hip.

Well, two can play at this game. I lift my arm and motion for her to back up. She frowns but does it anyway. I fight off a smile at the slight victory. I continue waving my hand until she moves far enough back. I try not to laugh at her tiptoeing backward through the mud in high-heeled boots better suited for a street corner than the woods.

"Thank you." It's gonna be a long week accommodating this gal.

I climb back in my truck and give Angie a thumbs up. She nods, her eyes wide as a coon's in a spotlight. I put the truck in reverse and give it some gas. Once Angie's car starts to tug, I hold up my thumb, signaling her to do the same.

And she does . . . just not how I expected.

She hammers the gas, throwing a steady stream of mud from her back tires. Blondie squeals from behind the car. I stick my head out the window and yell for Angie to slow down. She eases on the gas, and the car rolls out of the pit.

I get out and unhook the winch. When I raise my head, my eyes meet long, lean legs caked with mud. I follow them to a dirty skirt, then crossed arms, then a face full of disgust.

"Ma'am." I stand and tip my cap, trying to keep a straight face.

"Do you think this is funny?" She purses her bright-red lips.

I shake my head in a nonverbal lie. "I told you to stay back."

She rolls her eyes so far back that the green disappears.

"Excuse me." I slide past her. I catch a whiff of flowers as I do. It sure beats the smell of deer pee and raccoon poop. I haven't smelt anything that good on the property ever. Except for maybe the duck fart candles my cousin bought me as a joke. Turns out duck farts smell like fresh evergreens . . . according to the Country Candle Company.

I dip my head into Angie's window. "Okay, miss Angie, you're good to go. Just turn around and go beside the mud hole this time."

Her eyes fill with fear. "Do you mind turning it around for me?"

"Not at all."

Angie gets out and side steps along the edge of the road, keeping her eyes on the mud. Her shoes aren't any better-suited for the occasion than Blondie's, but at least they don't scream streetwalker.

I get in and maneuver the car around the mud, pulling it several feet past the danger zone.

Angie meets me at the door. "Thank you for your help."

"My pleasure." I get out and extend a hand. She hesitates, then shakes it, then blushes before getting in her car and driving away.

I turn to the other woman, still planted in the road as if the mud had cemented her. "Ma'am, if you'll get in the truck, I can get you to the lodge."

"I'm not walking back through that. You'll have to come get me."

I shrug. "Suit yourself."

In the time I lived in Tuscaloosa, I met plenty of city girls. But none were this stubborn. I trudge across the mud. Bending slightly, I tuck one hand behind her knees, the other behind her back. With one quick motion, I hoist her into my arms.

She lets out a small squeal. "I meant in your truck!"

"Well, that's where we're going. This is more efficient." I could annoy her as well as she could me.

I cock a smile. Then, I grit my teeth. She's a guest. A well-paying guest. And one for the first business conference I've ever booked. I need to focus on that. Not on how frustrating this woman brings much-wanted amusement to my mundane life. And certainly not how her slim body hugs against mine.

I carry her through the mud and open the passenger door to my truck. Still holding her in my arms, I manage to open the door. Then, I drop her in the seat. She lands with a huff.

"Uh, thanks . . . I think."

I laugh, no longer able to hold it back. "You're welcome." I slam her door and walk around to the driver's seat, then climb in. "And I don't think we've formally met. I'm Jack." I extend my hand.

She stares at my hand as if it were a poisonous snake. What's her deal? It's the same hand that cradled her legs a few second ago. After an awkward moment, she shakes it firmly. "Bianca Manderson."

I smile. "And now we've met." I back the truck up to the trees, and a low-hanging limb scrapes the cab. She flinches.

She sits like a statue while we make the mile-long drive to the lodge. I drum my fingers against the wheel and cut my eyes toward her now and again. She never looks my way, never says a word. Either I'm really that unbearable, or she still hasn't recovered from the mud bath.

I park in front of the lodge and turn off the truck. Out of instinct, I jump out and rush around to her side. I open the door to her hand in my face.

"I'm perfectly capable of getting out myself."

"I was simply opening your door, not carrying you across the threshold." I clear my throat and step aside. What was it about this woman that set me off so easily? Oh yeah, her evil witch disposition.

Remember she's a paying guest. Be decent.

She grabs hold of the handle on the side of the truck and lowers one leg toward the ground. The spike of her boot catches behind the running board, and she topples forward. I catch her and quickly realize my hands have landed on her rear. I slide them up to her waist as my neck starts to sweat. Maybe they weren't there long enough for her to notice.

"Easy," I say, warning for her not to try to jerk loose . . . but also as a warning to myself.

"I'm trying." She sighs and relaxes in my arms. A warmth rushes through my body. Oh, no. I don't need that. Not with Blondie. Uh, Bianca. I've lived alone in these woods too long.

I release one hand from her waist. "Lean against me."

Bad choice of words. She presses her head against my shoulder, sending the flower smell up my nostrils. The top of her hair tickles my chin whiskers. I grab the ankle of her stuck boot and maneuver it loose, then plant her on the ground before my senses overcome my common sense.

She straightens and pulls back from me but keeps her hands on my shoulders. Our eyes lock for a second, and I try to decide what color to call hers. "Green" doesn't do them justice. I've never seen a green like that in these woods. They're more of an emerald or jade or even some fancy color I don't know the name for. Peacock feather green. Is that an official color?

I blink and step back, giving her space.

"Thank you." She blushes, then drops her hands. She grimaces as they hit her skirt. "Eww."

I kick the side of my truck tire, trying to conjure up words to make this less awkward for her . . . and me. "I can get your bags and show you to your room. You can take a shower before the guys arrive, if you want."

"I'd appreciate that." Her bright red lips open to a smile.

So she is human.

I shut her door and retrieve the bags from my truck, then hand her the only normal-looking one.

"Thanks." She drops her phone inside and slings it over her shoulder.

I motion for her to go ahead of me, and I roll the larger bags behind us. They bounce over the loose gravel as I follow her to the lodge, holding in a laugh. Dirty handprints mark her backside where I caught her. Better keep that to myself.

CHAPTER TWO

Bianca

I raise my foot onto the first log step, more careful about where I place the heel of my boot this time. I've been felt up enough for today. Of course, none of it was intentional. I think.

I climb the thick steps, in awe of the building's beauty. I rub the soles of my shoes on the doormat. Before I can open the front door, Jack slides in front of me and opens it. What was with this guy? Must be part of his hospitality act. *That* I can live with. Lifting me into his arms and tossing me into a truck, I can't. Way too personal.

My eyes scan an entrance that is every bit worthy of a *Southern Living* cover story. The maple-colored wood with intricate detailing across the crown molding and beams. The vaulted ceilings and expansive lighting fixtures. Wait . . . are those chandeliers made of antlers? Interesting. But why would anyone build something so exquisite in the middle of a forest with no decent way in or out? Architecture like this belonged in Colorado Springs or at least the Great Smoky Mountains.

"Here we are." Jack smiles at me. He seems to mean well. I must admit I've never had a guy literally carry me out of danger before. Sure, he hadn't saved me from a fire-breathing dragon or even from some stuck-up guy in a sweater vest, like in a Hallmark movie. But him lifting me out of the mud without hesitation had lit a spark of hope I was sure had burnt out long ago. Maybe well-meaning men did exist.

I study his face as he shuts the door behind us. A swoony sensation I haven't experienced in years courses through my veins. I jerk my head forward toward the fireplace to focus on the lodge rather than him. Besides, lanky, unshaven men in overalls and rubber boots aren't exactly my type. And he doesn't have the best etiquette when it comes to words. I should really correct him the next time he calls me ma'am.

He takes a step away and props his hands on the tops of my bags. "What do you think?"

I tug my purse strap higher on my shoulder and nod at the fireplace. "The stonework is impressive. And this vaulted ceiling." I glance up, then turn to him. "I love it."

He blushes. "Thanks. That's the reaction I was going for." He taps the edge of my bag, then crosses his arms. "So, was it worth slopping through the mud?"

My muscles tense. "Why don't you ask me again at the end of the trip?"

He laughs. His eyes dance with every chuckle. They're the lightest blue I've ever seen. Almost transparent. Very complementary to his dark hair. Despite my best efforts to keep a straight face, my mouth starts to curve.

He clears his throat and removes his cap. "I'll give you the official tour later. I know you wanna shower and all first." I glance down at my mud-soiled attire. "Yes, thanks."

He leads me to a broad staircase. The ceiling, with carved log beams, draws my attention once more. We climb the stairs side by side, with Jack heaving the bags behind him. Maybe I shouldn't have packed so many shoes. But then I couldn't have enjoyed watching him suffer this way.

When we reach the top, he positions the bags on the landing and raises his arms in a victory pose. Or maybe in surrender.

My mouth betrays me once more with a slight smile. "So, which room is mine?"

"I gave you the room I give couples. That way, you'll have a desk and your own bathroom."

"Thank you." He'd given me the best room and had the forethought to understand I might need a desk or want more privacy. Most guys don't pay attention to such details. But it is his job to please guests.

He leads me down a long hallway with doors lining the outer wall. A railing along the left offers a view of the first floor. I admire the wooden beams even more from upstairs as we walk so close beneath them. Each one must weigh near a thousand pounds.

He stops at the edge of the hallway and sets my bags beside the door. "Here it is." He opens the door to what could best be described as a rustic honeymoon suite. A large four-poster bed, a stone fireplace, and a claw-foot tub, which leads to the bathroom entrance.

"Wow."

"Nice, isn't it?"

I nod and run my index finger down the doorframe. "What kind of wood is this?"

"Oak." He points to the fireplace. "And if you ever need a fire built, you can call me."

"Like, call the desk?" I scan the room for a landline.

"No." He laughs. "I'm not that legit yet. Use the number

you called before. It's my cell phone." He unbuttons the top pocket on his overalls and pulls out a business card that has seen its own share of dirt and grit. "Here's my official contact info."

I pinch the tip of it, forgetting for a moment that I too am covered in mud. It was simple, with only three lines of black text: Gamer's Paradise, Jack Jackson, and a phone number.

"Wait, your name is Jack Jackson?" I cover my mouth, muffling a laugh.

He sighs. "Yeah, my parents have a warped sense of humor. But hey, at least they didn't name me Jackson Jackson."

"Or Michael." I laugh louder, then clear my throat. "Sorry, I didn't mean to laugh."

"Yeah, you did." He slants his eyes.

I straighten and press my lips together to keep from insulting him further.

His mouth morphs into a playful grin. "Gotcha."

I let out a puff of air and relax. I'll have to watch myself around him.

"Well, I'll leave you to it."

I nod, and he walks out, shutting the door behind him.

After securing both door locks, I retrieve my toiletry bag and head for the bathroom.

The smooth wooden walls, which I now know are oak, carry over into the bathroom. The shower catches my attention right away as it is made from the same stone as the fireplace. I turn on the water and peel off my soiled boots, then do the same with my clothes. Aside from rush week in college, I've never been so filthy. I let my clothes fall in a pile on the floor. That will have to do for now. No way I'm putting mud into my silk garment bag.

I make a mental note to book a ride home in a four-wheel drive vehicle. Heck, I'd even allow a chauvinistic male smoker to drive me over getting stuck again. Which is probably what I'll find around here.

I stick my hand under the showerhead, sighing as warm water rinses dirt down the drain. My brightly painted nails reappear as the brown and red mud washes away. I step inside, never so thankful for running water. I lather my limbs twice with lavender spa soap. Just in case any kind of animal disease was mixed with the mud.

After a long shower, followed by my usual beauty routine, I thumb through my clothing. I pull out a pair of skinny jeans and a clean sweater. I choose my brown knee-high boots—the black ones would need a deep cleaning—and brush my hair back into a low ponytail.

There. That's as country as I get.

As I start down the stairs, multiple voices echo from below. Good. Being alone with Jack either makes me uncomfortable or way *too* comfortable. And I'm not quite sure how to process that.

I follow the voices into a room off the main living area. My eyes immediately settle on Jack.

"You must be Bianca Manderson."

I flinch at the voice beside me and turn around. An attractive middle-aged man extends his hand. I shake it and smile. "I am, and you are Macon or Ronald?"

"Macon." The man smiles back. "Ronald stepped outside to get cell phone service."

My heart sinks a little. That must mean no service inside.

"Don't worry. I can show you all the spots with the best signal." Jack raises his eyebrows.

I bite my tongue and work on flipping my frown. I need to play nice. Macon is watching.

A man a little older than Macon, wearing a cowboy hat, walks through the front door. He tucks a phone into the breast pocket of his flannel shirt. A huge grin crosses his face when he looks our way.

"Well, either this is Miss Manderson, or Jack is one lucky young man." He comes toward us and holds out a hand. "Ronald Elmore. The better-looking partner of Outdoorsmen Oasis."

I give his hand a firm shake. "Bianca Manderson."

"Now that we're all here, y'all help yourself to some food." Jack points to his left. "It's in the dining room."

We head in the direction of the dining room. A large wooden table with ornate legs takes up most of the space. The chairs have burgundy leather backing, similar to that of the couches in the living area.

"I always make my signature dish the first night." Jack beams. "Deer poppers."

I've never heard of deer poppers. Or deer anything. Are they cake poppers decorated like deer? I could go for that.

Once I step farther into the room, I notice food at the far end of the table. My face falls when I view the spread. Mud isn't the only thing here that reminds me of college rush week. Apparently, Jack's idea of hors d'oeuvres is Doritos and Oreos. And no cake poppers. Before I can protest, Dad's warning pops into my head. His angel etiquette trumps the devil diva whispering in my other ear. I plaster on my pageant smile and hang back while the men load up their plates with chips and cookies.

Jack disappears and returns a moment later with a large pan covered in foil.

"Fresh deer poppers."

My eyebrow raises. Maybe I would get a cake ball after all. He rolls back the foil, shattering all hope.

Stuffed jalapeño peppers. Gross. Both of the men grab one and bite into it instantly. My stomach churns at the greasy residue swimming in the pan beneath the peppers.

Jack tilts the pan my way.

"No, thank you."

"Oh, you've got to try it." Macon speaks between bites.

I swallow. The devil diva returns, as does my Dad's corporate wisdom. I hesitate, debating whether to politely decline the hideous grease ball or ruin my pampered palate for the sake of pleasing a potential business partner. "What's in those?"

Jack rests the pan on the table. "Not much. Deer meat and cream cheese stuffed into a jalapeño, then wrapped in bacon."

"Deer meat *and* bacon?" One of those alone could clog an artery. Given my family's high cholesterol and my desire to stay a size two, I can't justify eating it. Sorry, Dad. "Do you have anything more . . . green?"

Jack twists his mouth and stares at the pan. "You can have the one with the biggest jalapeño if you want."

Oh dear. This is going to be one long, hungry week.

Jack

I pull up a chair and pluck a deer popper from the pan. I sigh as I bite into one of life's simple pleasures. That magical mixture of meat and cheese with a hint of heat slides across my tongue and down my throat. My favorite family recipe. An easy treat Grandpa used to throw together every time we killed a deer.

Bianca sits across from me with nothing but a bottle of water. I motion toward the pan of deer poppers. "Are you sure you don't want one?" I wipe the back of my hand across my greasy chin. I should've put out napkins.

"I'm actually not all that hungry. Maybe another time." Her face creeps into a forced grin. Like when a dentist drills all over your mouth and then asks you to smile.

Despite being slim enough to blow away in a strong wind, she has to be hungry. She's been here for a few hours now, and I haven't stashed any complimentary snacks in her room. Or snacks in any of the rooms. Crap. I should add complimentary room snacks to my notes.

"Suit yourself. There's plenty." I offer her a smile. Her face remains tense.

"More for me, then." Ronald reaches across the table and grabs a handful for his plate.

I study Bianca's face as it evolves from fake smile to awkward frown. She clearly can't relate to these men. As the unofficial host, it's up to me to make this work.

"Macon, what kind of hunting supplies do y'all carry?"

"Oh man, everything you can think of. We also have fishing and hiking merchandise, but hunting is our bread and butter."

"Same here." I wink, and everyone laughs. A nervous laugh even seeps out of Bianca. I doubt she thinks I'm funny. Maybe she's trying to fit in.

"We have a lot of unique scent sprays I'm anxious to try out here," Ronald says, then licks his fingers and grabs more poppers.

"Scent sprays?" Bianca glances between Ronald and Macon.

Macon clears his throat after swallowing. "Sprays to mask your human scent and amplify the animal scents to draw in what you're trying to attract."

She raises her chin.

Ronald slaps Macon on the shoulder. "A simpler answer would be deer pee in a bottle."

Her eyes bug, and I almost bite my tongue off trying not to laugh. Ronald does laugh.

"I've got a lot to learn about this business." Her words came out in almost a whisper, as if saying them more to herself.

"Then you came to the right place." I wink, and some of the worry fades from her face. My gut twitches when she gives me a real smile.

"It'll be good to hunt around here. We need to see what supplies might appeal most to our eastern stores." Macon transfers Doritos dust from his hands to his shirt sleeve.

Oh yeah, napkins. I stand and cross the hallway to the kitchen. I snatch a roll of paper towels. What is it with me and forgetting napkins? Even though I market this place as a wilderness lodge, which it is, the whole intent in building a huge cabin was to give guests a luxury they normally can't find in the middle of the woods.

I walk back in to see Ronald hogging the last of the chips. "Sorry about that." I set the paper towels on the table.

"Thanks, man." Macon pulls one off, but Ronald sticks to licking his fingers.

"Do you carry any supplies for women and children?"

"Oh yes." Macon turns to Bianca. "We have a large inventory of outdoor clothing and shoes for the entire family. Supplies for first-time hunters and guns made specifically for women." His smile widens more with each item he names.

"Guns for women only?" She crosses her arms. Uh oh. Is she offended or interested?

"Oh yes. They're shaped better for a woman's grip. And some come in pink."

One of her eyebrows shoots up. "Why pink?"

"Makes them pretty," Ronald chimes in.

"I get that, but I'm more curious as to why everyone thinks women want pink."

Macon palms the back of his neck and turns to Ronald, then me. I shrug. This is their hole to crawl out of. I've dealt with her enough today.

"I mean, pink is pretty, but it's a bit juvenile and over-done to me. For instance, I like turquoise much better."

I snicker. That explains her eccentric baggage.

Macon squints his eyes and nods. "Hmm. I like that idea."

"I mean, I'm in no way an expert on your products, but it's just a thought. If you want to stand out, of course."

Macon smiles. "I like the way you think, Mrs. Manderson."

"Please, call me Bianca." She grins at all of us. "And it's just Miss."

I add that to my mental notes. Right after complimentary snacks. Not that her relationship status matters to me. Still, something about this city girl is intriguing. Sure, she needs a little meat on her bones and a bit of an attitude adjustment at times. But she can hold her own and has an independent streak I admire.

We talk a bit more, mixing in personal details with business. Ronald is a perpetual bachelor, which doesn't surprise me one bit. Macon proudly supplies a cell phone full of photos showcasing his wife and two college-aged sons.

After another hour and another tray of deer poppers, everyone migrates toward the living area. I build a fire, then locate the TV remote at Ronald's request. Macon settles into a recliner and gives channel suggestions to him. Bianca stands near the window, glaring at her phone. She holds it at a few different angles, then lifts it higher.

"Bianca, would you like me to show you the best cell phone spots while we tour the rest of the lodge?"

She meets my gaze and half-smiles. "That would be nice."

"Come on." I motion for her to follow me. Once she's by my side, I head toward the front door. "Do you have a jacket?"

"A light one upstairs. I didn't anticipate spending much time outside."

The irony of someone coming to a hunting lodge and not expecting to go outside baffles me to no end. Though I shouldn't be surprised since she's worn boots with spiky heels the whole time.

"Wait here." I go to the hall closet where I keep an emergency stash of coats and coveralls. I pull out the least-worn jacket I can find and bring it to her. "Here, you'll need this."

She frowns at the green Carhartt coat but reaches for it anyway. I imagine wearing something so simple is beneath her, but she'll appreciate it when the cold hits her.

I grab my own jacket from an antler hook by the front entry and flip on the outside lights. I open the door, and she walks onto the porch. I follow, closing the door behind us.

"Now, the first spot is where I park my truck."

"Is that why you park there?"

"No. It's the closest spot to the door." When you walk the woods as much as me, you want to avoid unnecessary steps.

We leave the porch and walk to the left side of my truck. "Here."

She stands beside me and holds up her phone. "Wow, it jumped from no bars to three."

"Yep, country magic."

Her green eyes lock on mine. They glisten in the moonlight. I turn away from her mesmerizing stare before my animal instincts kick in. We have nothing in common. More importantly, she's here on business. And her business has brought me business.

I clear my throat. "Okay, the best spot is around back." I

lead her around the back of the house. "Stay beside me so you don't step in any puddles from the gutters."

She moves close enough for me to catch a whiff of her scent. It's even stronger than before when I carried her across the mud. Her eyes trail to the gutters, then to the sky.

"I've never seen so many stars at one time."

"Really?" Even living in Tuscaloosa for a while, I could still see plenty of stars on the outskirts of downtown.

"Maybe once when I went to the mountains. But most of that trip was overcast."

I slow my pace and admire the sky with her. I often take for granted living in a paradise like this. A gamer's paradise, indeed.

"Here we are. Watch your step." I offer her my hand. Her soft, smooth hand soothes my calloused grip. A surge of energy shoots up my arm. Probably just the shock of her cold skin.

We walk across the slick stone patio to the edge.

"Right here."

She cranes her neck to the second-story porch above us. "So, a few feet beyond that upper deck."

"Yep." I forget we're still holding hands until she drops mine and reaches for her phone.

"Oh, four bars here."

"Yep, it's the best."

"And these are the only places with good service?"

I waver my head. "Pretty much, unless you want to take a trip several acres into the property."

"I think I'm good." She smirks, the worry now gone from her face.

I smile as I study her profile. I'll never understand why some women wear so much makeup. Especially when they don't need it. And she doesn't. A long moment passes. I feel weird for gawking at her so long. "Now, how about a quick tour inside?"

"Sounds nice. It's cold out here."

"Aren't you glad I had an extra coat?"

She nods, her lips forming a slight smile. "Yes, thanks."

We cross the patio to the back door. I nod to my right as I open it. "I can build a fire in that fire pit if you ever need to use your phone for a while."

Her smile widens as she brushes past me, sending a fresh stream of floral scent up my nose. Maybe the lady at Country Candle Company could bottle that scent for me. It's like a breath of fresh air this time of year.

I take her through the kitchen and the game room, then into the conference room. "This is where y'all can meet. I have a screen set up if you need it for your computers. And this big table, of course."

"This is really nice."

"You sound surprised."

"No." She shakes her head. "Maybe a little, but I don't mean that in a condescending way." She sucks in a breath, then exhales. "All this is a little out of my element. I had no idea what to expect."

I laugh. "No kidding."

"My dad usually handles these kinds of deals, but I'm branching out. Trying to expand."

"I understand that."

I can so relate to trying to expand. I'd ordered the screen and office chairs a few days after Macon booked this trip. Just after I'd decided on a whim to promote this place for outdoor lovers to hold business meetings. I also need this experience to go well.

Otherwise, I'd have to come up with more alternatives to drum up business. Deer and turkey alone wouldn't pay the mortgage.

CHAPTER THREE

Bianca

I wake up Saturday morning to a growling stomach. I haven't been this hungry since my friend Ariel convinced me to go on a week-long cabbage juice cleanse with her. No surprise why. The two bags of peanuts I'd stashed from the plane ride and eaten before bed hadn't exactly filled me up.

Maybe the kitchen has something decent to eat. I'm not sure how that works, as I've never stayed in a B&B before. If Jack makes deer poppers for breakfast, I'll consider leaving a bad review.

But first I need to clear my head. Not bothering to change, I climb out of bed and stretch my hands to my toes. I lift my arms and step out into warrior pose but can't concentrate with my stomach barking orders. Note to self: Next time, pack protein bars.

I get dressed and do my makeup. My first formal business meeting with the men starts in a few hours. That should give me time to go over their files and hopefully rummage up some food. Going down to the kitchen is still my best bet. Gamer's Paradise is presumably too far off the beaten path for ordering takeout. Plus, I hadn't noticed any restaurant signs on the way in, nor do I feel like walking to the backyard to order in food.

A whiff of bacon flows my way as I near the kitchen. Great. More fatty meat.

I stop in the entry. Beams of light dance through the kitchen's glass door panes and across the dark floor. Jack is at the stove, dressed head to toe in camouflage, whistling as he stirs something in a skillet. One of those heavy ones only used by cooking show contestants and cartoon witches. I walk toward the island and sit on a stool covered in animal fur. I squirm at the weirdness of sitting on actual hair, though it does make for a soft seat.

I slide a hand across the stone countertop, admiring its sleekness. Whoever designed this place could make a fortune decorating weekend homes in the Georgia mountains.

Jack puts on an oven mitt disguised as a fish and clamps the fish's mouth around the handle of the pan, then picks it up. He turns around and notices me for the first time. "Oh, hey, Bianca."

Surprising him gives me an odd pleasure. "Hi."

He half-smiles, then carries the smoking pan near the sink and starts moving meat to a plate. He still hasn't shaved his face.

"Are we the only ones awake?" I twist on the stool. It doesn't grip as well as leather, or cloth, or any normal stool material.

He laughs. "Hardly. We got back from hunting an hour ago. The guys are getting showers."

My eyes widen. "You've already hunted this morning?"

He pauses his transfer of meat and stares at me, spatula raised. "Yeah."

"Oh." I tap the face of my phone. "It's not even nine."

He laughs louder. "Which means my first quarter ends soon."

I shake my head. "I don't know anyone who'd do anything that early by choice."

He shrugs. "Most hunters enjoy the quiet of morning. There's something about starting your day in nature's peace."

I press my lips together. I enjoy nature by walking the beach. And even that doesn't happen until well after lunchtime. Beach. Ugh. Why couldn't these gun guys meet me in Florida, again?

"You didn't eat supper. You must be hungry."

"Oh, I'm not much of a deer and bacon kind of girl." I raise my eyebrows and lean back on the stool. A little too far, as I almost slide off. I grab the edge of the island to anchor myself. My stomach growls again. Should I rummage through the cabinets now or wait until Jack leaves?

"I'm about to cook eggs. You eat those?"

"Yes." I perk up. At last, a protein option I can live with.

"Great."

He opens the refrigerator and gets a carton of eggs. I try to sneak a peek inside before the door closes, but his bulky coat blocks my view. He sticks his hand back in the hideous fish mitt and places the pan, now void of bacon, back on the stove, then cracks an egg . . . right on top of the grease!

My stomach churns as eggs ooze around the bacon remnants. Jack resumes his whistling and gives the eggs a stir. He pulls some plates from the cabinet near his head and grabs forks from a drawer. After a few more stirs, he sets a plate in front of me and scoops a spatula full of eggs onto it, then hands me a fork.

I hold the fork, not sure what to make of the sloppy

mound in front of me. The eggs glisten with grease and smell like a Waffle House parking lot. I scrunch my nose.

"What would you like to drink?"

I take a deep breath, trying to center myself and keep cool. I should've done more yoga. But no amount of downward dogs could've prepared me for this. Maybe caffeine will do the trick. "Do you have coffee?"

"Sure." He crosses the kitchen and turns on a coffee pot.

I refocus on my greasy eggs. I flinch at the sight of them, but my stomach growls in protest. I've eaten so little the past two days. As much as it pains me to put something so toxic in my body, I cannot starve any longer. I reach for the roll of paper towels in front of me. Blotting off the visible bacon residue eases my conscience. At least a bit. I stab a piece of egg, then close my eyes before bringing it to my mouth. I chew generously to make the bite last as long as possible in case I can't muster another.

"How is it?"

I pop my eyes open to see Jack leaning across the island, inches from my face. Startled, I lean back and almost slide off the fur stool. "Tastes like bacon."

"I know." He beams broadly. "It's great, isn't it?" He taps the stone counter and pushes himself back. "The first time I did that, I couldn't believe I hadn't thought of it sooner. I mean, eggs are usually so bland."

And what was wrong with that? Eggs are healthy and predictable, just like I like them. It takes a special person to screw up an egg. And that person is Jack Jackson.

He turns his attention to the coffeemaker, and I sneak a few more paper towels to wipe down my eggs. I would not fall prey to my dad's high cholesterol. Nor eat like a Neanderthal on a Keto craze.

He brings over two mugs of coffee, both with handles shaped like antlers. First a fish mitt, now deer mugs. Where does he find this stuff? Probably the local Walmart. He tosses a hand towel over his shoulder and removes his cap, which is completely camouflage like the rest of him, except for the bright red Alabama football "A" monogrammed on the bill. He plops down on the stool beside me, effortlessly. I guess those camouflage pants have better grip than my skirt. A mixture of trees and bacon whiffs my way as he settles in his seat. Then he laces his fingers together and rests his forehead on them, closing his eyes.

He must be tired. Getting up before daylight to hunt, then cooking a ton of meat—I'm tired just thinking about it. But then I hear a muffled "amen."

I shift my attention to my coffee mug before he catches me watching him.

"Hey, you want something for your coffee?"

"I suppose you don't have almond milk."

He walks to the refrigerator and laughs. "I have real milk from a cow."

"Why do people say that?"

"Say what?"

I rest my elbows on the counter. "Allude to almond milk not being real milk."

He smiles. "Have you ever seen someone milk an almond?"

I open my mouth to say I've never seen someone milk a cow either. But realizing that isn't a valid argument, I simply respond with, "Good point."

He winks. My cheeks heat the same they did when he winked at me last night. He isn't flirting with me . . . is he? No way.

He brings over a gallon of full-fat milk and a bottle of vanilla creamer. "I also have this." He places both in front of our coffees and returns with a huge plate of equal parts bacon, deer meat, and eggs. He drops his head for a second, then lifts it, along with a fork full of eggs and meat. He shovels it all in his mouth at once.

"What?" he asks around the food as he chews.

I reach for the off-brand creamer as if I haven't just gawked at him. "Nothing. Just, you're rather slim to eat like that."

"I burn a lot of calories. And technically, this is all protein."

I shrug. "Do you have a spoon?"

"Uh huh." He hops up and grabs a spoon from a drawer.

"Thanks." I take the spoon from him and stir a generous amount of creamer in my cup. "Do you use this in yours?"

"No, I like my coffee black."

Of course he does. I lick my lips as Dad's horrid black coffee haunts my taste buds.

I sip my very beige coffee to kill the memory. No Starbucks, but it doesn't taste half bad for a creamer with a cartoon pig on the front. I swallow a huge gulp, and my stomach rumbles. I place a hand across my middle, hoping he hasn't noticed. Like it or not, I need to eat the eggs.

I fork another bite and close my mouth around it. Either the extreme bacon vibe wafting through the room is getting to me, or my hunger has overpowered my taste buds. But, somehow, I don't *hate* bacon-flavored eggs. Nor eating them beside a camouflage-clad guy with scraggly facial hair. But I wouldn't go as far as to eat them on a train in the rain, in a box with a fox.

Oh no. I'm seriously losing it.

Jack

I park my truck in front of the lodge and let Ronald and Macon out. They're all smiles, having enjoyed our afternoon hunt. "I'll take the deer and clean them. Make yourselves at home."

"Thanks, Jack." Macon shakes my hand before shutting the truck door, then the two men head inside.

I drive the short distance to my home, a modest cabin a few acres past the lodge. I back the truck inside my shop, where I clean and process deer. Chocolate and Brownie waddle up when they see my truck. I'm pretty sure they heard it coming even before they saw it. I pet both labs on the head.

They follow me to the back of the truck and sniff the air. Such groupies. I reach for the tailgate latch, then think better before lowering it. I best put the dogs in the house before bringing out fresh kill. As good as they are, I can't expect them to sit by with clenched jaws while I haul two deer out into the shop. I wouldn't dare torture my babies like that.

I lead the dogs into the house and grab a bag of treats from the kitchen counter. I toss one to each dog. Tails wagging, they gobble up the biscuits, then stare at me. I rub each one behind the ears a minute before heading back outside to finish the job.

I hang the first deer from a chain and close the shop door to block the wind. Then, I cross the concrete to the corner sink and wash my hands. As I soap up my chapped hands, my mind wanders back to when I lived in Tuscaloosa. Every chance I got, I'd come back here and hunt. This was my happy place long before my grandparents passed away and left the house and land to our family. My mom had mentioned on several occasions how I'd be better off to sell it all and return to my marketing career. All out of her so-called concern for me. I huff. She wants grand-kids . . . like, yesterday. And as an only child, I am her only shot.

At least my dad applauds me for wanting something of my own. From helping me get the land ready for business to doing all we could on our own to build the lodge, John Jackson has supported me every step of the way. Unlike Mother. Cleaning deer and managing green fields might not appeal to many, but I don't want to do anything else. Especially not sit in a cubicle making sales spreadsheets and social media ads.

After cutting, processing, and packaging the meat from both deer, I set aside the deer busts. My friend Roy offers discounts to the lodge's hunting guests since they make up most of his business. And having a skilled taxidermist who's local helps my business as well.

My chest swells with pride at the broad antlers on each buck. I've raised some mighty fine deer. These bucks will make nice mounts for Ronald and Macon's collection.

Once I clean up my mess, I go inside to clean myself. The dogs meet me at the back door, sniffing the deer on my pants and begging for attention. I pet them both on my way to the shower. It took some getting used to, living in my grandparents' old house, but after almost two years, it finally feels like home.

I step into the tiny square of bathroom and undress. I need to toss my clothes in the washer before heading back to the lodge or the dogs will lick them like a lollipop while I'm gone. I shrug. Ah, I'll just leave them there. Chocolate and Brownie deserve an unexpected treat to occupy their time. I turn on the water and duck under the curtain rod. Sometimes I shower at the lodge when I don't have any guests. This bathroom wasn't made for humans over six feet tall. Or over five feet tall, even.

I shampoo and soap, then scratch at the dried deer blood on my hands. Blood and mud swirl in a rust-colored stream down the drain. I stand beneath the shower head until the water falling from my body runs clear.

I hop out, nearly taking out my neck on the curtain rod when I do. Good thing the cheap plastic isn't painful. I grab a towel from the wicker rack above the toilet. One day I'll replace it with a practical metal bar. But Grandma had proudly displayed lacy towels and bowls of potpourri on it most of my life. I guess I'm a little sentimental about the rickety thing. I rub my wet hair with the towel and glance in the mirror. The fog fades, revealing my scruffy chin. Most years, I embrace "no-shave November" as the perfect excuse to wear scruff for the rest of the winter. I run a hand across my prickly cheek. Maybe I need a more clean-shaven appearance for hosting professional guests.

Not for Bianca.

Still, I can't ignore the way she stares at my chin.

Why do I care what she thinks of me? Of course, I want her to like me for the sake of our business situation. But why should my looks matter?

I start combing my hair, then sigh. I put the comb down and reach for the shaving cream. May as well. What can it hurt?

Thirty minutes later, I've changed into jeans and a flannel shirt, fed the dogs, and started back toward the lodge. Time to start dinner.

The guys and I have eaten plenty today. Lots of protein for breakfast and plenty of snacks on the afternoon hunt. But Bianca hasn't eaten more than a plate of eggs. Unless she's secretly indulged in my offerings of Doritos and snack cakes, which I highly doubt.

I park in front of the lodge and pull up Mrs. Mary's Diner in my contacts. I hit the call button and wait for an answer.

"Mrs. Mary? Jack. Could you send some salad stuff when you deliver the potatoes and beans?"

She laughs and asks if I'm kidding. Mrs. Mary has helped feed my guests for well over a year now, and I've never ordered salad.

"No ma'am. I'm trying to broaden my menu." I drum the steering wheel as she laughs again. "And if you have any of your banana bread or bran muffins, send those too. I can use them for tomorrow's breakfast."

To my relief, she has a fresh cake of banana bread. Maybe Bianca can eat that for breakfast.

"Thanks, Mrs. Mary." I hang up the phone and run a hand across my drying hair. I reach for my favorite Bama cap and start to put it on, then take a good whiff. Whoa. Straight up deer pee and pine straw. Probably not a good idea to set that on my clean head.

I drop the cap in the passenger seat and head for the house. As I enter the kitchen, faint voices echo from the conference room. With any luck, I can have supper ready by the time their meeting ends.

I retrieve the pan of steaks I marinated earlier and line them on the grill right outside the kitchen door. Trial and error has taught me to prep things. I've come a long way since the days of burning microwave burritos. Of course, at the time, I lived a few miles from fast food tacos. Out here, it pays to know how to cook a few things. And for what I couldn't cook, I had Mrs. Mary.

As if she's read my mind, Mrs. Mary pulls her van beside the patio. She gets out carrying a box of food. I inhaled the home-cooked aroma. "I was just thinking about this. Thanks."

"You're welcome, sugar." Mary hands me the box. "I gave you some of my house dressing for the salad."

"Thanks." I smile. Maybe Bianca will like it. I'd just as

well eat store-bought ranch. "Let me get you a check." I motion with my head for her to follow me inside.

About the time I sign the check, voices ring out from the hallway. I rip the check from the book and look up. The men and Bianca are at the far end of the living room. I hand the check to Mrs. Mary, who's focused on the living room. She turns to me. "I see why you wanted the salad now."

"Yeah, they're staying a few days longer than most guests."

She cackles. "I was referring to your lady friend in there."

"Oh." My ears heat up. "She's not . . ." Surprised at my squeaky tone, I clear my throat. "She's here to meet with them."

"Mm hmm." Mrs. Mary grins and pats me on the arm. "Let me know how it goes."

I sigh and run a hand through my hair. "Don't they need you back at the restaurant?"

She laughs louder and wiggles a plump finger at me as I follow her out the back door. "Quit acting all concerned about my business just so I'll get out of yours."

"Okay." I laugh and wave as Mrs. Mary climbs into her van and drives off.

🦌

I carry all the food to the dining room and put out a stack of plates and forks. And a roll of paper towels this time. Thanks to the list of reminders I made last night. As I uncover Mrs. Mary's famous mashed potatoes, a whistle lets out behind me. I turn to find Ronald standing in the doorway.

"Man, that's a nice-looking spread."

"Thanks. I had help from the diner in town. Y'all come fix your plates while I get some drinks."

Ronald nods. "Appreciate it."

Not as much as I appreciate his business.

I walk toward the kitchen and meet Bianca standing at the counter. "Thanks for the salad."

I palm the back of my neck. Why does everyone automatically assume it's for her? "No problem. Just trying to add a little green to the jalapeños."

She raises an eyebrow. "Funny, I don't see any deer poppers tonight."

"That's because it's my traditional welcome dinner. Guests only get that privilege their first night. And sometimes at departure."

She smirks. "Oh, how clever."

I go to the refrigerator and pull out a jug of sweet tea and several bottles of water. "Well, I used to work in marketing."

"Really?" Her nose wrinkles as if she thinks I'm joking.

"Seriously. My degree's in marketing."

"You have a degree?"

I set the drinks on the counter and huff. "I'm not some braindead hillbilly."

Her jaw droops. "I didn't mean that. I just—"

"It's okay." I swallow. I shouldn't take out my pent-up frustration on her. "Not everyone thinks I made the best decision moving out here and opening the lodge. That's all."

She brushes her blond hair to the side and nods. "Do you need help with anything?"

"You can take these drinks to the dining room while I get ice."

"Sure." She reaches across the counter for the waters, brushing her side against my arm. Heat shoots through me. I step toward the cabinet and away from the flowery scented woman in the tight skirt.

She rounds up the waters with one arm and grabs the tea with her other hand. I watch from the corner of my eye as she exits the kitchen. Instead of tall boots, she has on regular high heels—which perfectly show off her toned calves. My eyes drift upward and settle on her tight black skirt. I blink, forcing myself to stop checking her out. Yes, she's hot. But not my type. Well, maybe just the exterior. But what's under the hood could use some work. Not worth my time.

My eyes lock once more on her calves. Ugh. It's just a pair of legs. I really need to get out more instead of spending so much time with four-legged females.

I take a second to collect myself, then carry glasses of ice to the dinner table. Everyone has fixed their plates, so I do the same. Ronald and Macon are at one side of the table and Bianca sits across from them. I hesitate. Should I sit on the end? But with only four people at the table, that would clearly indicate that I don't want to sit by her. And I am a grown man, not a middle-school boy. Besides, she has no reason to think I like her in that way. So far, most of our interactions have ended in sarcasm. I set my plate beside hers and slide into the chair next to her.

I dip my head in my hand for a quick, silent prayer. I still haven't figured out the protocol for praying with guests around. Will they care if I pray aloud? Not wanting to offend anyone, I always opt for what I call a headache prayer. Capping my hand over my forehead and tilting it down as if I need to massage a migraine. I'm in the business of camou-flaging things, so it makes sense.

Once I recover from my "headache," I cut into my deer steak and glance at Bianca's plate. Potatoes, baked beans, and salad. Everything but deer. My body relaxes as she eats without hesitation. I should've ordered extra salad for tomorrow.

"Jack, do you play cards?" Ronald asks between bites of his second steak.

"Mainly poker."

"Well, what else is there?"

Everyone laughs.

"You up for a game with us tonight?"

"I could call some friends. See if any want to ride out here. Make it a little more of a challenge."

"Oh, I'm plenty enough challenge."

Macon shakes his head. "He's all talk."

Ronald scowls. "I've got twelve more years of life and way more bachelor days than you. Factor that in, and I've played way more poker than you, and obviously Jack."

Macon lifts, then lowers a shoulder. "True."

Everyone laughs again. I slump back against my seat. Bianca eating a full meal and warming up around the guys means I'm doing my job to bring everyone together. At least for tonight. Now, if I can just talk her into going outdoors with them and wearing something other than skin-tight skirts.

For practical reasons . . . and to hide those long, toned legs of hers.

Bianca

I sit back and smile. My stomach is full for the first time since I arrived in Apple Cart. For a town named after apples, it sure is hard to find actual fruit. But Jack has made an effort to bring in some veggies, which both surprises and pleases me.

After dinner, the men agree to retreat to the game room, and I go to my room. I change clothes and check my phone for the first time in hours. One missed call from Dad. I groan at the thought of jogging back downstairs to make a call. Instead, I go on the balcony connected to my bedroom. It overhangs the patio where I'd gotten four bars of cell service earlier.

I stand in the center of the balcony and check my phone. Nothing. I hold it a little higher. One bar. For a few minutes, I stroll around, repositioning my phone in search of a better signal. At the edge of the balcony, two bars appear. I raise my arm over the railing, close as I can toward the spot below with the four bars.

Three. That should work. Too bad the bars disappear as soon as I pull my arm back. I wrinkle my forehead. Ugh. Think, think, think . . .

What if . . .?

I change my audio to speaker and tap Dad's cell contact. I hit the call button and stretch my arm far as I can over the railing. My armpit stings as I push my arm out farther.

It's ringing! Perfect.

"Hello."

I yell toward the receiver when Dad answers. "Dad, it's me."

"Bianca?"

"Yes, I'm calling you back."

He says something else, but it comes through muffled. I grip the phone tighter and raise onto my toes. I shove my hips against the railing and bend over as far as I can safely.

"Dad, can you hear me?" I speak even louder this time.

"Say that again."

The man is too proud to break down and buy a hearing aid. I've told him repeatedly that anyone who proudly wears Benjamin Franklin frames shouldn't mind a tiny clear bug in his ear.

I lean a bit farther and grunt as my hip bones cut into the wood railing. "Dad!"

"Is everything okay?" A voice calls from behind me.

I bounce down on the balls of my feet and spin around, dropping my phone over the balcony in the process. Jack. Did he barge in on all his guests like this?

I clench my teeth and glance back toward the railing, then at Jack. "No, I'm not okay. But I dropped my phone."

"And you thought yelling at it would help?" He scratches his now cleanly shaven chin.

I plant my hands on my hips and scowl. "No, idiot. I was on the phone yelling at my dad, and I dropped it when you scared me."

"Why were you yelling at your dad?"

I throw up my arms and sigh. "Because he couldn't hear me. And I had the phone on speaker because I had to lean over the railing to get a good enough signal."

"That's not safe. Something could happen."

"You think?" I pinch the bridge of my nose. I'm in no mood for obvious accusations.

"Do you want me to help you find it?"

"That would be nice." I don't even try to hide my sarcasm.

We walk back into my room, and I close the patio door behind us. As I scan the floor for my shoes, I spot my black push-up bra hanging from the back of the desk chair. My heart stops momentarily as I cross the room, snatch it by the strap, and sling it under the bed. Maybe he didn't notice.

Nope. The smirk on his face says it all. Just great.

I drop my eyes as my cheeks warm with embarrassment. I push my feet into my shoes and tighten the bun on top of my head. "Let's go."

The mischievous grin stays on his face halfway down the stairs. At last, he speaks. "Do you know where you dropped it?"

"Somewhere near the side of the good signal spot."

"Why didn't you just come downstairs and call?"

I huff. "Please, enough with the whys."

"Okay, I'm sorry."

I raise one corner of my mouth in an attempt to hide my irritation. We go to the kitchen, and Jack flips on the outside light. Then, we go outside to the magical signal spot.

I look up and down the patio. "I don't see it."

"Maybe that means it didn't hit the stone."

I kneel at the edge of the patio and pat the grass around me. Jack squats beside me. The light highlights his face. His jaw is more chiseled than I'd expected it to be under his whiskers. And he has thick hair, especially for someone who wears a cap all the time.

"Anything on your side?" He tilts his head, leaving only a few inches between our faces.

My muscles tense. My body heats up despite the cool breeze. I focus on his face. So handsome without stubble and a cap to hide it.

"Do you see it over there?"

"What . . .? Oh, the phone." I jerk my head down and pretend to search for it. "I don't see it over here."

Jack stands and walks forward. I hang back out of his view so he can't see the embarrassment I'm sure is written all over my face.

"Wait." He squats again, this time by a mud hole at the edge of the stone. "I found it." He lifts the phone. Mud drips from the screen.

I stand slowly, my heart sinking deeper with every inch I rise. "Oh, no."

"It's okay. I've had phones get wet before."

"With mud?"

He nods. "Yeah."

I inhale and exhale deeper than a chain smoker. So much for trying to impress Dad on this trip.

"Let's go clean it up." Jack heads back inside.

I trail a few feet behind him. I swallow as my eyes narrow in on his backside. Guys in Atlanta wear skinny jeans but not like these. They complement him well. Very well.

"Oomph." The side of my face slams into the glass door. I stagger back and rub my throbbing head.

"Are you okay?" Jack clutches my arm and pulls me against him.

My mouth goes dry and my pulse races. "I . . ." I clear my throat. "I wasn't watching where I was going." That was the understatement of the year.

"Let's get you inside." He squeezes me closer and leads me through the door, shutting it behind us.

Now I have two pulses racing. The one in my heart and the one in my head. But something about having his arms around me helps numb the pain.

"Here, sit down." He eases me down onto a furry barstool.

I grip the island counter to steady myself, as my yoga pants don't exactly agree with the animal hair. Jack stays behind me, his chest pressed against my back. I lean forward to put some space between our bodies. He drops his hand from my arm and circles the island. I'm both glad and sad for him to move. He bends over and opens the cabinet under the sink. I bite my lip and focus on the deer antler light fixture above my head rather than his backside. I can't make that mistake again.

"Here we go."

I slant my eyes to make sure it's safe to look. Whew. Jack is standing now, holding two Ziploc bags. He wets a towel and wipes down my phone, then sets it aside before filling one bag with rice and the other with ice. Whatever he has in mind, I sure hope it works.

"This is for your phone." He drops my phone into the bag of rice and seals it. "We'll let that dry out overnight." He wraps a dry hand towel around the bag of ice. "And this is for your head."

I take the ice and hold it against my forehead. The coolness stings at first, then soothes my throbbing temple. "Thanks."

"You're welcome." His lips curve into a slight smile.

"Here." He reaches across the island and centers the ice on my head.

I hold my breath as his hand wraps around mine. That same sense of comfort I got when he held me against him rushes over me. His hand lingers a moment, and our eyes lock. I rub my parched lips together, halfway wishing he would kiss them. As if literally reading my lips, he leans in ever so slightly. My stomach jumps. He's going to kiss me.

"Who do we have here?" An unfamiliar voice calls from the kitchen opening.

Jack drops his hand from mine and straightens. I jolt back to reality. And not a moment too soon since kissing Jack would make no sense whatsoever. I twist on the stool. A brown-haired guy around our age is propped against the doorway. He's wearing a button-down shirt a size too small and a smug grin.

Jack crosses his arms and backs away from me. "This is Bianca. She's here to work with Macon and Ronald."

"Lucky them." The guy grins wider, if that's even possible, revealing perfect teeth.

"And, Bianca, this is my friend Tanner. One of our poker players."

Tanner puffs out his chest and strolls over to us. "Tanner Nash." He extends a hand.

I set down the ice and shake his hand.

"Whoa, what happened here?" He drops his face close to mine. A little too close considering we've just met. And considering he isn't Jack. Judging by his expression, my head has started to swell.

"I accidentally ran into something."

"That's the commotion I needed to see about." Jack winks at me. Heat trickles down my spine.

"Oh, no wonder we heard yelling." Tanner laughs and sits on the stool beside me.

My face heats up again. I didn't anticipate anyone hearing me yell at my phone. At least Jack didn't mention my literal dropped call. I snatch the bag of ice from the counter and push myself to standing while I still have a shred of dignity intact. "I think I'm going to take a bath and call it a night."

Tanner stands and raises a hand. "Don't go on my account."

"No, I'm just really tired. It was nice to meet you."

Tanner takes my free hand between both of his and holds it for an eternally awkward second. "The pleasure was mine. Best of luck with your business."

"Okay." I wiggle my hand free and wave my fingers, signaling him to leave. He backs out of the kitchen, stopping at the arched doorway. "You coming back, Jack?"

"In a minute. I'm going to make some snacks first, so start this hand without me."

Tanner nods, then waves at me before disappearing behind the wall.

Jack and I exchange smiles.

"I apologize. He's a bit of a ladies' man."

I laugh. "So I see."

"Well, if you need anything, you know where to find me. I'll let you rest." Jack knocks his fist on the counter and goes to the pantry door.

I want to leave, but my feet won't allow it. Even though I shouldn't, something urges me to stay with Jack a little longer. As I sit contemplating whether to stay or go, he returns with a box of honeybuns. "You need something else?"

I fumble the bag of ice between my hands, thinking of an excuse for sitting here. "You said you have snacks?"

"Yeah, in a minute. I've got to grill them."

"Oh, deer poppers?" If that's the case, I'll need to come

up with a different excuse to make my staying with him in the kitchen believable.

He laughs. "No, grilled honeybuns."

"Grilled . . . honeybuns?" My eyes focus on the box.

"Don't knock it till you try it."

I shrug and follow him onto the back patio. He lights the grill and unwraps several snack cakes. Then, one by one, he places them on the grill.

"A few minutes on each side, and they're good as golden."

I stand close enough for warmth but at a safe distance for him to flip the honeybuns. His light blue eyes glisten in the light of the grill flames. A few minutes later, he removes them and grabs a bottle of water sitting beside the grill. He douses the flames, sending smoke out. I cough and follow him inside.

"Now what?"

"We cover them in ice cream."

I instinctively lick my lips. He laughs, then pulls out a stack of bowls and puts a honeybun in each one. I help him scoop ice cream and add spoons.

"Take yours to-go and rest." He hands me a bowl. "Remember, if you need anything tonight, find me."

I nod as he balances the remaining five bowls on a platter and leaves the room. Armed with a snack cake concoction in one hand and an ice bag in the other, I climb the stairs to my room. I curl up in a hunter green throw and taste the treat. And what a treat it is.

As I indulge in more sugar than I normally eat in a week's time, my mind drifts back to Jack. Warm and cozy with a bowl of ice cream, and I still prefer having Jack soothe my banged up head.

But why?

Jack

Last night has thrown me for a loop. I'd come close to kissing Bianca and would've had Tanner not ruined the moment. I can't decide whether I love or hate Tanner for that. Or whether I love or hate Bianca.

Definitely more love than hate for Bianca.

After she went upstairs, I spent the rest of the night trying to get her off my mind. Was her head okay? Was she worried about her phone? Did she enjoy the dessert? And was she thinking about me too?

Having her on my mind led to two things: the worst game of poker I'd played since college and the best sleep of my life. I haven't drifted off with a woman on my mind in a long time. Not that there haven't been women who wanted to take up residence in my head . . . and heart.

When I moved back from Tuscaloosa, it sparked the radar of all respectable single women of marrying age in Apple Cart. So many women stopped by to "welcome" me, I wouldn't doubt the local PD had put it out across the scanner. From college girls home on break to single moms in their early thirties—the full range of them had brought me a welcome dish of some sort. And the ones too old to claim me for themselves still brought food, along with suggestions of younger women "just perfect" for me. Usually their grand-daughter or a girl from church.

I'd eaten dang well my first few months back. But once I started sending the dishes back by my cousin Jonah instead of in person, the women got the hint: My interest didn't extend beyond a full belly. I did eventually go on a date a time or two—as initiated by my mother. But none of those set-ups materialized into anything more than a few dinners. I haven't felt a real attraction to anyone in years. Until a couple of days ago when I carried Bianca across the mud, like the happy ending to some redneck fairytale.

I pull on khaki pants, a button-down shirt, and my good pair of boots. I don't plan on coming home before church, so I feed Chocolate and Brownie, then check on the baby deer behind the house. One little doe requires bottle feeding and another needs to be moved to a pen with its mother.

After that, I put the bottle back in the shed. I eye two guns that I haven't shot in a while resting in the corner. They need to be shot, and I have enough time to run a round or two through each while Macon and Ronald finish their breakfast. I load them in my truck and head toward the lodge.

Last night replays in my mind, making me smile. Bianca had started off snarky when I'd questioned her yelling, but then we connected on a deeper level. Joking and sarcasm aside, I enjoyed helping her way too much. To the point that I was glad she'd dropped her phone and almost glad she'd run into the door. Okay, maybe not the last part. That's rude. But it had given me a chance to hold her close.

I park a few acres back from the lodge, where I've set up some targets against a dirt bank. I plan to expand this space later for an actual shooting range but haven't done so yet. I grab the first gun and hop out of the truck. Excitement rushes through me as I load it. Few things satisfy me like firing off a good gun. I get out and open my toolbox to find more bullets. Score! I not only find bullets to fit this gun but also a little bottle I've been saving for target shooting. I hold up the bottle and shake it. The tiny balls bounce around like pop rocks in an eighties' kid's mouth. Mix in a little powder and these will make one heck of an explosion. Ronald will love it.

I finish loading my guns and mix the concoction in an

empty Coke bottle rolling around the bed of my truck. Then, I position the bottle in front of the dirt mound, step back, and plug my ears. I square my shoulders and center my eye on the scope.

I pull the trigger, releasing a bullet . . . along with all the pent-up tension from fighting my attraction to Bianca. A deafening blast vibrates the dirt as colored dust blows in multiple directions.

Guns. The perfect solution to girl issues. Or any issues, for that matter. I fire off a few more shots, then hear a scream from the trees out past the mound.

I lower my gun and head for the line of pines. The trees rustle ahead of me. Moments later, Bianca stumbles out, red-faced and breathing heavier than a deer in heat.

"Did you shoot at me?"

I stare at the rifle in my right hand. "I shot." I look back at her. "Not at you."

She sucks in a breath, then shakes her finger toward the trees. "I was right back there"—she pokes the finger at my chest—"and you shot there!"

I clench my jaw. Turns out shooting guns is a solution to combatting my attraction to Bianca. Just not in the way I'd originally thought.

"No, I shot the dirt." I step over to the mound and pick up a shell. "See?"

She lets out another long breath and wipes her hand across her forehead. "When I asked about exercise equipment, you said I could run on this trail."

"Yeah, and it looks like you did." Heat rises up the back of my neck. I twist the shell between my thumb and index finger, squeezing it hard enough to start a pulse in my fingertips. "I aimed at this dirt pile. It wouldn't go into the woods." I toss the shell at the bank. "I'd never shoot randomly at the trees like that. We have hunting areas for a reason."

I return the gun to my truck and slam the door. "I'm going to check in with the men before I leave." Too mad to drive, I march back toward the lodge.

Bianca rushes up behind me. "Leave?"

"I'll only be gone a few hours."

She speeds up to meet my pace. Her face has mellowed from the mix of rage and terror. "I'm sorry I accused you of shooting at me."

"That's okay. It's not the first time a woman's accused me of that."

Her green eyes grow about an inch wider.

So what if it was in third grade when I'd snuck a slingshot to school? She didn't need the fine details. I smile and raise my hands in surrender. "I'm kidding."

She presses her lips together and frowns. "Not funny."

But it was. I laugh, and I don't feel bad about it. Not after she acted like I'm some hitman on the hunt.

We walk up the patio and through the back door together. Ronald and Macon are on barstools, finishing off plates of steak and grits.

"Was that you shooting?" I've barely shut the door before Ronald asks.

"Yeah."

"Tannerite?"

"Yep." I wink as Ronald bursts out in laughter.

"Aw, I told you Macon." He pats Macon on the shoulder and laughs himself into a cough. He clears his throat and turns up his coffee cup.

I walk to the coffee pot. "More coffee, anyone?"

"I'll take more, thanks." Ronald coughs once more and slides his cup across the island.

"I'm good." Macon takes a sip from his cup. "Thanks, Jack."

Bianca strolls toward me. "I'll take a cup." She turns to

lean her back against the countertop next to me. My limbs are numb. Her floral scent is now mixed with pine and sweat, which attracts me even more. I go to the island and grab Ronald's mug, thankful for a reason to move away from her alluring smell.

Crap. I've gone full-on animal instinct for this woman. Calm down, cowboy.

I position my back to Bianca and refill Ronald's mug, then start a new pot for Bianca and me. "I've got to leave for church service soon, but I'll be back before lunch. You men are welcome to use the side-by-side while I'm gone if you want to go hunt."

"Appreciate it." Ronald nods as I set the fresh mug of coffee in front of him.

"So that's why you look nice?" Bianca's words come out almost in a whisper.

I turn to find her staring at me. "So, you think I look nice?" I raise my eyebrows and grin.

Her face flushes, but not out of anger this time. She uses the same finger she'd shoved at me earlier to fan in front of me, indicating my clothing choice. "I meant how you're dressed."

I lift my chin. "Yes, I don't do camo at church." I wink. Her cheeks blush even more, and it excites me to know my actions have that effect on her.

She tucks a stray hair behind her ear and drops her eyes. I turn back toward the guys, who are too focused on their grits to pay any mind to the conversation going on behind them. Good thing.

I lift my voice to get their attention. "Does anyone need anything from town?"

"Town?" Bianca perks up like Chocolate and Brownie at the word "treat."

"Yeah, my church is on Main Street."

"I'm fine," Macon mutters between sips of coffee. Ronald shakes his head.

"Would you mind taking me by the market to get some groceries?" Her face lights up, and I'm certain visions of broccoli and kale dance in her head.

I shrug. "Sure."

"Great, let me go grab my purse." She bounces out of the kitchen, her yoga pants highlighting every curve of her body.

I chastise my eyes for checking her out. Maybe I need to shoot the gun a few more times before I get in my truck with her.

I sigh heavily. Good thing I'm headed to church.

Jack

I open the passenger door to my truck for Bianca. She flinches at the two rifles propped barrel-up against the console.

"Hang on." I pick them up and carry them to the back door on my side, then place them on the gun rack in my back glass. I make sure to not point the barrels her way, even though neither is loaded. Then, I climb in my seat.

She slides into her seat, still wearing those spandex pants I need to ignore. She reaches behind her, lifting her hips from the seat. "Uh, here." She has a box of shells in one hand and my Bible in the other.

"Thanks." I put them on top of the console. An easy way of reminding myself not to ogle her legs.

But in my defense, she is the first female guest at Gamer's Paradise to wear yoga pants. Or to come without a significant other. So, other than gluttony from leftover honeybuns, I haven't yet faced much temptation in this occupation.

Until now.

I run a hand through my hair and clear my throat. "Church should only last an hour or so. I hope that's okay."

"Yeah, sounds good."

We drive in silence most of the way. But not uncomfortable silence. As I turn on the main road leading into town, my neck starts to sweat. The whole community will see Jack Jackson driving around a pretty blond wearing Black Widow britches. Not good. Not good at all.

I park in front of the Piggly Wiggly. With most everyone in church about now, she should have no trouble finding whatever she needs. Unless she needs something organic, unknown at the Pig.

"Okay, take your time. I'll be back before noon. Brother Johnny tries to let us out in time to beat the Methodists to Mrs. Mary's."

"Mrs. Mary's?" Bianca scrunches her forehead. "Everyone gathers at the same woman's house?"

I laugh. "Mrs. Mary's Diner. The restaurant a few blocks back."

"Oh." Bianca twists her head to look down the street. "Why did the sign say 'Diner'?"

"Long story short, when Mrs. Mary bought it, she couldn't afford to change the sign. She wanted to name it something cool like 'Mary's Home Cooking.' But the sign said 'Diner.' Pretty soon everyone started calling it 'Mrs. Mary's Diner,' and it stuck."

"Hmm." She nods. "Do you happen to have a Publix or a Target nearby?"

I shake my head and fight off a laugh. "Sorry, but this is it."

"Your only grocery store is a place called Piggly Wiggly?"

She hesitates saying "Piggly Wiggly" as if she has trouble pronouncing it.

"Unless you count the dollar store and the gas station. But neither of those have much green." I nod toward the front of the store. "I promise you, next to my hunting grounds, this is the freshest meat you'll find for miles."

"And if I don't want meat?" Worry lines take over her face.

"They have plenty of vegetables. And vegetable oil."

Bianca nods and picks up her purse from the floorboard. "Thanks." She opens her door and hops down. "Have fun at church."

I nod. "Have fun going green." As soon as she disappears between the automatic doors of the Pig, I rev up the Dodge, signaling my personal rebellion against going green.

And I don't even make it out of the parking lot before a few people smile my way. Not a neighborly "how are you" smile, but one of those "I saw you with a girl" smiles. Well, church should be fun.

I keep my eyes on the road as I drive the short distance to Apple Cart Baptist Church. People file in the front door as I park in the back near the other larger trucks. The vehicles transition into vans as I near the entrance to the children's hall. I slow my pace in hopes of strolling in right before service. This isn't a day I care to engage in small talk.

I make it in unscathed and slip into the end of the back pew. Brother Johnny preaches a good sermon as usual, and the choir sounds nice. The girl who used to make me lasagna sings a solo. Maybe I should add venison lasagna to the lodge menu.

The worship leader makes a few announcements, then Brother Johnny dismisses us in prayer. I stand and start toward the door as soon as I hear "amen." But not soon enough.

Ms. Ethel and Mrs. Maudy corner me on the front steps.

"Hello, Jack." Ms. Ethel pushes her walker closer to me, daring me to try to run.

"Hi, how are you ladies?"

Both of their faces light up like Christmas. "The real question is who was that young woman you left at the grocers before church?"

I stare at the floor and wish it would swallow me up. Word spreads fast in Apple Cart, but this gossip has set some kind of record.

"How did . . .?" I look up, then shake my head. I don't even want to know. "She's part of a business conference taking place at my lodge. She needed a ride into town. That's all."

Mrs. Maudy straightens her glasses and stares at me as if trying to read my mind.

"Well, I need to go get that young woman back to her meetings. You ladies have a nice afternoon." I hurry down the porch and make a beeline for my truck before any more questions come my way.

Now to navigate the Pig without any interrogations about my personal life.

As usual, more cars populate the grocery parking lot now that churches are ending their morning services. I park as close as I can to the front and watch the sliding door. After three songs come and go on the radio, I sigh and turn off the truck.

I shove my hands in my pockets and rush inside. It shouldn't be hard to find Bianca. Most people around Apple Cart don't shop in yoga pants. They either dress like debutantes or make a midday run in their pajama pants, nothing in between.

Oh, and she doesn't have a southern drawl. I hear her

before I spot her. Sure enough, she's in the produce aisle. Big surprise there.

"But it doesn't say if these were grown without pesticides."

I shake my head. Bianca is holding a head of broccoli in one hand and propping the other on her hip, grilling some poor stock boy about pesticides.

"It's okay. I can help her."

The boy waves a hand at me and ducks his head before rushing back toward the storage area. Poor kid.

"Bianca, what's the deal?"

"I don't know if this is truly organic." She fans the head of broccoli in front of my face. "It's just setting there under the sprayers. No labels."

I slap my forehead and try not to laugh. "That's because it's fresh from the farm next town over." I pick up an apple from the bin beside us. "And these came from the orchard down the road. It's all fresh." I return the apple and grip her slim shoulders. "Trust me."

Her face widens into a smile. "Okay."

I give her shoulders a squeeze before dropping my hands. For a moment, I forget how much I don't need to touch her and how much everyone in town doesn't need to see me touching her.

Bianca tears off a plastic bag from the spool near the sprayers and sticks the head of broccoli inside. She adds it to her buggy. I follow her toward the checkout.

"You know, for someone who ate a honey bun last night, you're acting awfully picky about ingredients."

She elbows my ribcage side.

"Ouch." I laugh as I rub where she poked me.

I help her put her groceries on the belt, glancing around now and again in the hope that nobody sees us. The cashier adds the total. Bianca reaches into her purse. I put my hand on her arm to stop her.

"I'll get it."

"I can get it."

I pull her arm out of her purse. "You're a guest at my lodge, and food is part of the package."

She starts to talk, and without thinking, I hold a finger up to her lips. They are as soft as I imagined.

"Don't. I've got it." I slide my finger from her lips, already having left it there too long, and pull out my own wallet.

I count out enough money to cover the cost and hand it to the cashier. She grins at me and then at Bianca. All of a sudden, my mouth tastes sour. I really shouldn't have touched Bianca's lips.

And now that my hands know their softness, I'll have a hard time keeping them from my own lips.

Bianca

A week ago, if someone had told me an attractive outdoorsman would take me shopping at a place called Piggly Wiggly, I'd have laughed to the point of peeing myself. But here I am. Not peeing myself, but still at "the Pig," as Jack calls it.

We wait as the automatic doors slide open, exposing us to the wilds of Apple Cart. Jack walks to my side when we reach the truck and opens my door. "Do you want these up front with you?"

"Yes, thanks." I have come to anticipate him opening

doors. And perhaps he's come to anticipate me not wanting my belongings in the back of the truck.

I reach for the oversized handle above my head and climb inside. He hands me the paper bag of food and shuts the door. A few people pass by, each one craning a neck my way. I know nothing about small towns except what I've observed on TV. And if that's correct, any outsider coming in is a big deal.

Jack gets in and shuts his door. He turns his head to back up, then locks his eyes with mine as he faces back toward the windshield. "Would you like something to wear besides workout clothes and business clothes?"

I run my hands down my yoga pants and tilt my head. Is this his way of saying he doesn't approve of my clothing? Because until today, I haven't exactly been a fan of his wardrobe. Well, except for maybe those cowboy jeans that nearly gave me a concussion. "Like what?"

He shrugs. "Something you wear outside if you decide you want to. Boots without spikes."

A laugh escapes my lips. "Spikes? You mean heels?"

"Whatever."

I stare down at my yoga pants once more. Maybe he has a point. Dad wants me to find some common ground with these clients. Macon and Ronald wear jeans and boots all the time.

"What do you have in mind? That boutique I saw on the way here?" My cheeks lift at the anticipation of shopping someplace without a pig on the wall. I'm in much need of some retail therapy. The clothing in the window is from last season . . . but still.

"It's not open on Sundays. And I don't think they have what you need."

My grin drops, taking my shoulders down with it. Half of this town shuts down on Sundays. Not a good marketing plan, if you ask me. "Okay, if you think it will help. I'm always up for shopping."

Jack grunts and shakes his head.

I squint. "What's that mean?"

"I didn't say anything."

I try my best to imitate his grunt. I sound like a constipated cat. "That's not saying anything."

He half-smiles but keeps his eyes on the road. "You didn't look too happy shopping in the Pig."

I huff. "Clothes are fun. Food is a necessity."

He chuckles. I want so badly to stay frustrated at him. But he makes it hard when he laughs. His whole face lights up, and his eyes get even lighter. If that's possible.

Before I can say anything else, he turns off the road into a gravel parking lot. He pulls up in front of a metal warehouse of sorts. My stomach burns. Please don't be a second-hand store. The only thing worse than wearing unattractive clothing would be wearing unattractive clothing someone else has previously owned.

He turns off the truck and motions for me to get out. I put my hand on the door handle, then hesitate for moment, thinking Jack will come open the door. When he doesn't, my rib cage tightens as if I've endured a small tragedy.

After overcoming the slight shock of opening my own door, I drop my feet to the ground and stare at the tall metal structure in front of us. Lawnmowers line the front entrance, and a chalkboard sign reads, "Boot Sale."

My eyes trail toward the top of the building. An old wooden placard is hung at a crooked angle. Like maybe it started falling and nobody bothered to climb up and fix it. "General Store" is carved and stained into it. Beneath that hangs a slightly smaller metal sign—still at a straight angle. "From cradle to coffin?" My spine shivers as I read it aloud. What kind of place is this?

Jack laughs as he circles the truck to my side. "It's their slogan, meaning they have everything you need, from an infant until . . ." He makes a gagging noise and scrapes his index finger across his neck.

I raise my chin and try not to laugh. Keeping a straight face would best communicate that I'm not amused with his choice of, uh, clothing store.

He opens the front door to the building and waits for me to go first. I smile to myself. Chivalry isn't dead, after all.

We walk in to a big shelf of fake flowers bulging out to our left. I feel like Alice in Wonderland braving the talking garden. Except these flowers are the kind old people put in those small concrete vases on gravesites. I push a fake rose out of my face. "I guess they weren't kidding about the coffin part."

Jack shakes his head. "Nope."

I swallow as my eyes dart around the room. As if reading my mind, he reassures, "But they don't have actual coffins. The local funeral home has the monopoly on those."

My body eases. "Good to know. So where's the clothing?"

He leads me past lawn equipment, animal feed and supplies, kitchenware, and an entire section dedicated to John Deere. Apple Cartians must live strange lives. Aside from the kitchen utensils, I could go to my own coffin before needing any of this stuff. The back wall of the store holds one of the largest inventories of boots I've ever seen. And I've seen a lot of shoe stores. But a quick glance tells me these boots aren't my type.

Jack leaves my side and walks to the far corner of the room. I twist my mouth, curious as to what he'll have me try on. I rock on my heels and pray that none of the few people milling about try to strike up a conversation with me.

A minute later, Jack returns with the most stylish pair of cowboy boots I've ever laid eyes on. Or should I say cow*girl* boots. Squared toes made of tan leather meet a turquoise leg with a floral pattern embroidered with shimmery, brown thread.

"How about these?"

I blink to make sure this isn't a mirage, as I'm in obvious need of a fashion fix. "They're gorgeous."

"Yeah?" He taps the toe on the boot and smiles. "I thought they looked like you."

A warm sensation runs down my limbs. Is that his way of saying he thinks *I* look gorgeous? He likely means they look like something I would like. I reach for the boot.

He hands it over and brushes his fingers against mine. Our eyes lock, and I linger, not wanting to lose his touch. His strong, rough hand gives me an odd comfort.

"Hey, Jack, can I help y'all with somethin'?"

I jump and turn to see an older man wearing a rather eccentric western shirt and stonewash jeans. This must be how cowboys dressed in the 1990s.

"Hi, Mr. Paul. My friend likes these boots." Jack nods at the boot, then drops his hand as if he's forgotten we're touching.

When his hand drops, so does my body heat. I shudder at the instant chill of breaking contact with him. "Uh, can I see these in a size seven?"

"You sure can, darlin'." Paul clicks his tongue and points at the boot. "Let me borrow this." I hand him the boot and stand back as he struts through the door to the stockroom.

I gaze around, impressed at how with dozens, if not hundreds, of options, Jack picked the perfect pair of boots for me.

"Jeans?"

"Hmm?" I face Jack, getting lost in his blue eyes.

"Now you need jeans."

Jeans. The view of Jack's tiny tush waltzing in front of me flashes through my brain. I close my eyes and breathe deeply.

"You okay?"

My eyes pop open. "Yeah."

Jack tilts his head toward some clothing racks behind us. I go over and fan through an array of jeans. Different shades of denim, some more embellished than others. I select a few pairs in my size.

"How about this?" He holds up a simple white button down shirt from the rack beside mine.

I shrug. "Are there any coats?"

"Plenty." He drapes the shirt over his arm and leads me to a rack of coats. All of them resemble Jack's coat I borrowed during the cell service tour.

"Hmm, any ladies' coats?"

He selects a grayish-purple coat from a rack. "This is the ladies' section."

My eyes bug. Why would any woman voluntarily choose to wear something like this? Forget fifty shades of gray, these coats came in fifty shades of brown. Oh, and full-on camouflage. Lovely.

"Okay, darlin'." Paul lifts a box over his head as he comes our way.

I turn my back on the unattractive coats and focus on the one Atlanta-worthy piece of clothing in this entire store. Turquoise boots.

Jack

I prop my elbows on my knees and unlock my phone. I shoot Macon a text to let them know I'm bringing food home for lunch. After that, I click on my security camera app to check on the game cams.

Two cameras in, a screeching noise raises the hairs on my arms. I lift my head to the shower curtain pulling back on the single dressing room. Bianca steps out and examines the curtain she's just moved.

My jaw drops, and I almost flop out of my folding chair. I've now seen her in hooker boots, a tight skirt, and painted-on pants. But she's never looked more attractive than right now, wearing a simple white shirt, jeans that fit in all the right places, and boots that make sense.

"Why is there a tag hanging from this curtain?" She fumbles with the shower curtain.

I snicker. "Paul will sell anything not bolted down." She scrunches her forehead. I nod. "Seriously. I once watched him sell the belt buckle he was wearing to an amateur rodeo rider."

"That's strange." She lets go of the curtain and steps back to face the one full-length mirror at the back, which also has a price on it. "How do I look?"

That's a loaded question. What can I say? You're the most beautiful woman to blow through here in years? Thank God we found you some functional shoes? Nothing seems appropriate, so I play it safe. "Nice."

"Nice?" She crosses her arms and scans the mirror for flaws.

Uh oh. I've played it too safe. "Very nice."

"Oh, thanks." Her eyes roll with more force than the Crimson Tide.

I scratch my chin. "I love you in that." Love? Why the heck did I say *love*? I swallow, expecting her to chastise me or take it as sarcastic.

Instead, her green eyes twinkle, and her lips curve into a sweet smile. One of genuine appreciation. "Thanks."

"You're welcome." I return the smile, and her cheeks blush. She ducks her head and disappears behind the flowered vinyl curtain.

I suck in a deep breath. I should be at Big Butts BBQ by now picking up lunch. Instead, I'm teaching a fashionista how to dress for the real world. Worst of all, I don't mind it one bit.

Why do I enjoy spending time with a food-snob city girl who's never set foot inside a general store before?

The metal curtain rod screeches again, and Bianca walks out wearing her own clothes. She holds the boot box in one hand and the clothing folded in the other. "Do you mind if I borrow the coat you lent me on Friday night?"

"Not at all."

"Good. I don't want to buy something I'll never wear again." She strolls toward the jeans. Instead of putting back the pair she's tried on, she grabs another pair like them.

I lift my eyebrows and study her as she goes to the rack of shirts and selects a black one like the white one I picked out for her.

"Okay, I think this is enough." She heads toward the front of the store. I stand, still a bit shocked at her agreeing to my clothing suggestions.

She sets everything on the front counter, right beside a bucket of fly-flaps. She frowns at the bucket and reaches for her purse.

My chest tightens when Paul scans the boots. "I can pay for those. I know they're kinda pricey." I don't want her to spend a lot of money on account of my suggestions.

She laughs and waves a hand in my face. "Please. Most of my shoes cost twice this much." My eyes widen. Mine sure don't.

She fishes out her wallet and hands Paul a card. "Besides, this is already starting to feel like a reverse *Pretty Woman*."

I raise one eyebrow, afraid to ask exactly what she means by that.

We exit the store prepared for Bianca to go outdoors. Well, as far as clothing is concerned. Now I need to teach her how to stay calm around rifles.

I drive up to the barbecue trailer down the street and park the truck. "I'm gonna pick up some food for lunch. Would you like anything in particular?"

Her mouth gapes open as she cranes her neck to read the sign. "Big Butts BBQ?"

"Yep, best smoked wings for miles."

She shrugs. "Why not?"

"That's my girl." I wink at her before opening her door. As I walk to the trailer, I shake my head. I have to stop winking at her. Every time I do, she blushes, sending a surge of heat through my veins.

Most of the after-church bunch have come and gone, but a small group of people are standing by, waiting on ribs. I notice them eyeing my truck and whispering. No doubt, they've spotted Bianca. I give it two days tops before my mom calls to ask about my new girlfriend.

I come back to the truck with two large bags. As soon as I shut the door, the smell of smoked meat overwhelms the interior. I back up and drive down Main Street. When the post office comes into view, I remember I need to get my mail. I turn in and park. "I'm going to run in and check my box really quick."

She nods while scrolling through her phone. She's probably taking advantage of the decent service in downtown before we head back to the lodge.

I go inside and pull the small key from the fold in my wallet. I unlock my PO box and pull out the contents. A catalogue for deer stands, some coupons from the Pig . . . I could've used that an hour ago. And one more envelope that makes my mouth go dry. I know right away what it is . . . and who it's from.

And unlike the covered dishes and the girls who'd brought them, these letters never stop coming.

CHAPTER SIX

Bianca

First, Piggly Wiggly, then the coffin slogan store, followed by smoked wings for lunch. Of course I should shoot a gun. It fits with the theme of the day: try something new.

I have to admit, those smoked wings were delicious. Even if I didn't slather them in ranch salad dressing like Jack suggested.

I change into my new clothes and admire my boots. They'll go perfectly with my denim skirt back home. I pull my blue fleece over the white shirt and check my hair in the mirror. After running on the trail, then rummaging around town, my makeup could use a touch-up.

After a few swipes of mascara, some lipstick, and a spritz of perfume, I feel more like myself. Riding home with all that barbecue has infiltrated my signature scent.

I head downstairs and out onto the property. I find Jack where he shot at me earlier this morning. Okay, so he hadn't been aiming at me. But no matter what he says, the shots did come my way. I heard them loud and clear.

Jack has the tailgate of his truck down with enough ammo spread across it to defend the Alamo. Ronald and Macon are standing off to the side with their own guns. Outside of watching police dramas, I've never seen so many guns in one place. And never at all in real life.

"Hey, come here." Not until Jack speaks do I realize I've planted myself at the bottom of the hill, as if staying close to the house will somehow protect me.

I creep toward Jack, my hands gripping the edge of my fleece.

"Here." He shoves some hideous orange headphones on my ears. Then, he reaches for a gun. "This gun won't hurt you. It's light and easy to shoot. The gun I learned on." I stare at his face to read his lips, as the headphones have muffled his voice.

I turn my attention to the gun barrel and stare at it for a long moment. At last, I nod and muster a nervous grin. My hands quiver slightly as I position the gun like Jack instructed. He must have noticed my shaking, because he stands behind me and places his hands on mine.

"Tighten your shoulders."

I swallow. I am tight. That is until he moves behind me and wraps his arms around me. I melt against him quicker than ice cream on a hot honeybun. I lift my shoulders and try to concentrate on the fact that I'm holding a gun for the first time. Not that an attractive guy has his body against mine.

Jack mutters something about how to hold my shoulders and brace myself. But my focus is on his hands cupping mine and his chest rising and falling against my back. I swallow harder and pull the trigger. My heart skips a beat at the noise.

"Did you blink?"

"Yes . . ." More like I shut my eyes. But that can qualify as a long blink.

"How about we try it again with your eyes open."

Easy for him to say. I've never touched a gun until now. And somehow, he expects me to hit a circle of paint on a dirt hill. I shake out my trigger hand, then resume my stance.

"Remember, I'm right here. I won't let anything hurt you."

His words wash calmness through my body. I lean into him, positioning my arms like he said, and pull the trigger. My eyes stay open this time.

I gasp as the center of the dirt circle puffs up dust. "I did it. I shot the dirt!" I raise my hands and hop, accidentally firing another shot in the air.

Squealing, I drop the gun and leap into Jack's arms. My heart beats eighty miles a minute as I bury my head in his chest.

"Whoa. Rule number one of gun safety. Never jump around with a loaded gun." He eases me down to the ground. I stare at him a moment before letting my hands fall from around his neck. His eyes sparkle as he brushes a stray hair away from my face.

A gun fires beside us, reminding me that we're not alone. Part of me wishes Macon and Ronald would leave, but the more sensible part of me appreciates having unofficial chaperones. Otherwise, I might have kissed Jack.

A large boom sends a shiver down my spine. Blue powder flies across the dirt pile, and Ronald cheers. My heart leaps into my throat, like it did at the shot that almost took me down in the forest.

Jack wraps an arm around my shoulder and rubs my shoulder blade. "It's fine. Just a loud noise, that's all." I nod and lean into him. His touch brings my heart rate back to normal. "And I think that's the last of it, anyway."

I look up at him. He smiles down at me. "Want to shoot again?"

I nod. He drops his arm from around me and bends to pick up the gun. I drop my eyes and mentally warn myself. Focus on the gun, not Jack's backside. My life might actually depend on that in more ways than one.

He repeats the instructions on how to hold the gun. I remember everything but fake a few false starts so that he'll put his hands on mine. Then, I fire another shot into the center of the dirt. My eyes widen, and I squeal in delight. I bend my knees to jump but freeze mid-squat, not wanting to repeat my last mistake. Except for maybe the part where I ended up in Jack's arms.

"That's good, Bianca." Macon walks up beside us. He plants his hands on his hips and examines the target. "Hey, you should go hunting with us in a minute."

"I don't know . . ." My voice cracks. I have literally just shot a gun for the first time ever. "I don't even own any camouflage, and you saw how I dropped the gun."

"Now that the initial excitement of your first shot is over, you'll be fine." Macon waves his hand dismissively. I find the casual way he downplays my misfire rather disturbing. Not at all how someone who sells guns for a living should respond.

I turn to Jack, searching his eyes for an answer. Instead of speaking, he steps closer so that our faces are almost touching. Then, he sniffs me.

"You smell like roses and honeysuckle."

I cock my head to the side. "And that's a bad thing?" According to all the perfume counters in Atlanta, it isn't.

"Bucks are finicky and much smarter than you'd think. They know those scents aren't natural to this season."

I frown. "So I can shoot a gun, but I can't go into the forest because I smell too good?"

He laughs. "When you put it that way, yes." He removes

his camouflage cap and runs a hand across his thick hair. "Why don't you shower. I'll get you some camo to wear as well."

I grit my teeth. Weren't showers for when you smelled bad, not good? I glance at Macon, who's now a few feet back comparing guns with Ronald. I need to prove I have an interest in their company, their business. And that requires finding common ground, like Dad advised. And what better way for me to do that than to go hunting?

"Give me half an hour?"

Jack nods, his handsome face forming a smile so big that it brings out the faint wrinkles around his eyes. I return his smile, though less enthusiastically, and un-suction the muffs from my head. I hand them to Jack and start toward the house. I make it almost to the back patio before Jack yells out behind me.

"And don't put on makeup or deodorant."

I freeze. I wear makeup any time I leave the house. I'm in shock at the thoughts of perspective clients—and Jack— seeing my naked face. I imagine scaring them into shock, then flinch when something taps my shoulder.

Jack is now by my side. He holds up a lock of my hair to his nose and inhales. "Your hair smells good, too. I'll let you borrow my unscented shampoo and deodorant."

Well, that explains why the man always smells like pine trees and mud. Even this morning, he'd been scentless until we both bathed in barbecue smoke. Hey, there's an idea.

"Can't I just lock myself in your truck a while and let the smoke knock the roses off me?"

He sneers. "You need a shower."

I narrow my eyes so he can't see them rolling back in my head. We walk inside together and climb the staircase. Jack stops at the first door past the landing. He opens it to reveal a massive storage closet with tons of toiletries.

He grabs a few bottles and hands them to me. "Shampoo, deodorant." I inspect the simple labels. Jack straightens from rummaging in the closet. "Sorry, no makeup. The women who come here to hunt always bring their own unscented makeup."

I tilt my head to the side. "That's a thing?"

He nods. "Yeah, I had this couple here last week, and the woman found hers online. She was a lot like you."

"What's that supposed to mean?" I put a hand on my hip and watch Jack's neck redden.

"Uh, pretty?"

"Mmm hmmm."

"You know, likes to fix up."

My lips twitch. I can't stop them from forming a grin. I enjoy teasing Jack and watching him squirm. "So, you think I'm pretty?"

"No."

I wrinkle my forehead. That's a bit forward for a guy who was blushing and stammering a second ago.

He steps within inches of me. "I think you're beautiful."

I swallow the heat pulsing through my body. Nothing but sincerity lingers in his eyes. The redness in his face disappears, and his eyes fall to my lips.

Jack leans in and brings a hand to my face. His touch is calloused but comforting. Strong, unlike the soft hands of men in Atlanta. A real man's hand.

My cheek heats up as he caresses it with his thumb. I study his handsome face as it closes in on mine. My eyes flutter shut as his lips gently close on mine. Good thing he shaved that scruff yesterday, or I'd need some extreme facial cream to remedy beard burn.

His hand migrates from my cheek to cradle the back of my head as he tilts his own head to deepen the kiss. His other hand rests on the small of my back. I drop the shampoo bottle and slide my hands up his chest.

I've dated—and kissed—a lot of men. But even the hottest, richest playboys in Atlanta didn't have an effect on me like this country boy. My muscles relax as Jack snuggles me closer. He kisses me even more passionately. Then, without warning, he pulls back and drops his hands.

I blink, unsure of why he stopped. Then, I turn to see Ronald topping the stairs.

"Hey, no judgement here. If I were thirty years younger, Jack wouldn't stand a chance."

My stomach bottoms out. My already flushed face reaches a heat advisory warning. I slide my hands down Jack's chest and wipe them on my jeans as if I can wipe away the kiss that easily.

"I'm sorry." Jack speaks to Ronald, but then slants his eyes toward me.

Was he sorry we'd gotten caught, or sorry he'd kissed me at all?

Jack

One guest catching me kissing another guest can't be good for business. Bianca slinks down the hall and into her room like a school girl caught with the wrong guy. This leaves me alone with Ronald.

"Ronald," I scratch the side of my head, trying words out in my mind before choosing which ones to speak. "I've never kissed a guest before. That was unprofessional, and I—"

Ronald holds up his palm. "Son, I get it. I was young

once, too. And even an old bachelor like me can see what's going on between the two of you."

My nerves loosen, but not to the point of unraveling yet.

"And don't worry, I won't say anything to Macon. Not that he would care."

Another knot unties in my stomach. Thank God Ronald understands my need to not let anyone else know about the kiss. The fewer people who know, the better.

"Thanks, Ronald. I can assure you it won't happen again."

Ronald gives me a quick nod, but something in his eyes reveals disbelief. He half-smirks and pats me on the shoulder as he passes by toward the bathroom he shares with Macon.

I exhale a huge breath of air I'd been holding in since ending the kiss. I hurry downstairs and find Macon still outside. Good. That means he couldn't have overheard—or overseen—the kiss debacle.

"I'm gonna run to my house and change. I'll be back in a few minutes, and we can load everything up."

"Sounds good." Macon cocks the gun in his hand and continues shooting at dirt targets.

I hop in my truck and drive to my own cabin. Chocolate and Brownie meet me at the truck door. I reach down and pet both an equal amount, then collect my mail to take inside.

After giving both girls a treat, I sift through the mail. I toss everything except for the one thing I want to toss. Or shoot. Like a dog walking into the veterinarian clinic, I get tremors every month when this letter arrives. I set it on my desk in the corner of the living area. Since it's already past due, I can put it off at least until tonight.

I start toward my bedroom, stopping a moment to pet the dogs as they chew on their treats in the center of the room. Their tails wag, but they're too busy to want to follow me.

I flip on the light and change out of my church clothes. When I worked in an office, my wardrobe consisted of ninety percent khakis and ten percent camo. Now that ratio is flipped. And I prefer it that way.

I change and then dig out an old pair of smaller coveralls to lend Bianca. I wore them when I was younger and not quite as tall. And just in case she forgets—or rebels—and uses her flowery shampoo, I grab a bottle of deer pee from on top of my gun safe.

Not long after I make it back to the lodge and load the guns, Bianca comes out wearing her new clothing, but no makeup. I stop in my tracks and stare. She doesn't need makeup at all. Without all that shiny stuff on her eyelids, the green in her eyes gets all the attention. Her skin is smooth and creamy as ever. And her light pink lips make me want to kiss her all over again.

Ugh. Calm down, Jack. Not an option.

I duck my head inside the truck and grab the coveralls. I can't keep looking at her lips and not think about our kiss.

"Here." I hand her the coveralls, making sure our hands don't touch.

"Thanks." She unfolds them and holds them up.

"Wear those over your clothes. They should fit decent and keep you warm."

She smiles. She strolls over to a patio chair, removes her boots, and puts them on. After zipping the coveralls and putting on her boots, she stands and faces me as if wanting my approval.

"Perfect." The word comes out more suggestive than I mean for it to. I clear my throat. "Perfect fit."

"Thanks." She drops her eyes and runs a hand down her side.

"Let me get some water and snacks, and we can go."

I pack a cooler of water and a duffle full of chips and honeybuns. I put them in the second side-by-side, since the guns take up space in the other.

"Okay, we're ready to ride. One of you can drive the other vehicle and follow me."

Ronald sits in the passenger seat of the second vehicle, obviously not wanting to drive. Before Macon can claim the spot next to him, I slide into the driver's seat. That will leave Macon to drive Bianca. And give me an excuse not to be near her.

Not that I don't want to be near her. The problem is that I very much do want to be near her.

We head out onto the trail leading to my favorite hunting spot. I've added space heaters and chair cushions to this roomy shooting house, making it the most comfortable on the site.

I park off to the side of the stand, and Macon pulls up beside me. We unload everything in silence, and each man takes an armload up the ladder. Then, I climb back down to help Bianca up.

She frowns at the house. "I've never climbed a treehouse before."

I bite my tongue to keep from laughing at her calling it a treehouse. "But you've climbed a ladder, right?"

"Once. When decorating for a Junior League fundraiser at the hospital."

I nod. "I'll stay behind you."

"Thanks." She grins widely, highlighting her high cheekbones.

I follow her and wait as she steps up the ladder. She climbs a few rungs, then hangs like a sloth on a branch.

"What's wrong."

"I don't like heights."

"It's okay. I'm behind you." I step up to the ladder to make that statement true, even if it does position her backside dangerously close to my peripheral view.

She climbs two more rungs and reaches the base of the shooting house. When she throws one arm over the platform, her balance slips, and she starts backward. Her camo-covered bottom flies toward my face, and I have no choice but to catch it.

My hands shake as if they're holding a wad of stolen cash. "I'm so sorry."

"Don't be, you saved me." The desperation in her voice suggests I've rescued her from a boatload of pirates rather than keeping her from falling five feet.

Clenching my jaw, I manage to keep my cool and hoist her into the opening. She lands with a huff and pushes hair away from her face as I climb in behind her.

"So, this is where you spy on deer?"

"Yep." I wipe my hands down my pants and motion for her to have a seat.

I open my camera bag and mount the recorder to the edge of the house.

"What's that?"

"I record all the hunts and give the hunters a video when they leave."

"That's a good idea." She settles into her folding chair and peers through the window opening.

I enjoy watching her waver between curiosity and boredom as she sips a bottle of water and picks at her painted nails. About an hour into our conversations surrounding Outdoorsmen Oasis, leaves rustle in the distance. A huge buck creeps into the clearing. Macon lifts his gun and drops it with one shot.

Bianca lifts her shoulders and scoots to the edge of her seat for a better look.

Ronald holds a pair of binoculars to his face. "Man, Macon. Looks like he's at least a twelve pointer."

"Only one way to find out." I stand and nod toward the opening. "Come on, Macon. We'll get a picture of you with him."

Macon and I exit the house one at a time and go to the deer. He circles around to the side of it, examining where the bullet went in, while I count the tines on each antler. "Thirteen points." I call out loud enough so that Ronald can hear.

"That's a nice deer." Macon strokes it's back before holding up its antlers.

I back up and take some photos with my phone. "Yep, you'll get a lot of meat off this boy." I peek around the phone, estimating the amount of meat I can salvage from it.

I back up one of the vehicles, and Macon helps me roll the deer onto the attached loader. Then, he lifts it. "I can take this back if you guys want to hunt more before the sun sets."

"That'd be great." Macon strokes the antlers one last time, his face beaming with pride. Then, he climbs back into the shooting house.

As I secure the deer, Bianca starts down the ladder. With her back to the steps, she eases down. I watch, wondering if she wants to see the deer. For all I know, she's never seen a real deer up close before.

Once both her feet hit the ground, she brushes her hair behind her ear and stares at me. "Can I get a ride back?"

I hesitate, trying to ignore the flames pulsing up my neck. "Uh, yeah." I wave my arm toward the passenger seat. "Come on." As she rounds the front to the passenger side, I slant my eyes toward the shooting house. To my relief, Ronald is keeping a straight face.

I really don't need to kiss Bianca again, and riding through the woods alone will make it hard to avoid.

CHAPTER SEVEN

Bianca

I climb into the vehicle and hold onto the bar in front of me. I've never cared for riding without doors. Jack stares ahead, focused on the trail.

"Thanks for taking me back."

"You're welcome." He answers in a monotone voice without looking my way.

The wind whips inside, so I inch closer to Jack. I wish he'd wrap an arm around me to help me stay warm, but he doesn't act interested. I let go of the bar and cross my arms, sacrificing my safety for warmth.

We ride in silence past the lodge and the dirt mound where we shot earlier today. A minute later, Jack backs the vehicle up to a large metal building.

"Jack." I can't stand the silent treatment any longer. "What's wrong?"

"Nothing." The corner of his mouth crimps into a pity smile.

"No, something's odd. You're too quiet."

He stares down at his lap and sighs. "I'm sorry for kissing you earlier. You're a guest, and it was very unprofessional of me."

"Oh." I blink. The only thing I was sorry about was Ronald coming up the stairs. That was possibly the best kiss of my life. "There's no need for you to apologize."

"I talked to Ronald after you went to your room. He isn't going to say anything and didn't seem to care."

I nod.

"I hope I didn't make things awkward for you with him, or with me."

"No, you didn't."

He breathes deeply and cups his hand around the bill of his cap. "Bianca, I'm not usually the type to come on to women like that."

My cheeks and shoulders start to shake as I repress a laugh. How cute. Of all the chauvinistic males in Atlanta, Jack couldn't dare offend me with a sweet kiss. But his eyes beg me to answer.

I don't want to compare him to the guys I know all too well. Forget apples and oranges. This is like contrasting calamari with deer meat. Each has its strengths, so it comes down to whatever a person prefers.

My eyes glare into his, sad and beautiful. I have an answer for him, and with any hope, he'll accept it.

Without saying a word, I lean in and press my lips against his. His lips stiffen. I draw back and search his face. His eyes have a hint of fear and shock, as if he's afraid to kiss me back.

I need to treat this like a business deal. If the client doesn't know what he wants, it's my job to show him.

I wrap my arms around his neck and kiss him again. This time with passion, like he kissed me earlier. After a few seconds of negotiating, he tilts his head and returns my kiss. A few seconds after that, his hands rest on my back and pull me closer. We continue the kiss a little longer, but not near long enough.

I'd gone on a date the week before coming to Alabama and had a decent time. So it wasn't the company of a guy causing me to swoon like a prep-school girl at her first coed mixer. It was *this* guy.

Jack dips his forehead to mine for a second before straightening in his seat. He licks his lips and clears his throat. He's blushing. How adorable.

"So I take it you weren't offended by me kissing you earlier." One side of his mouth cocks into a slight grin.

I laugh. "Quite the opposite."

He does that thing where he removes his cap and plays with his hair. "Bianca, I'm conflicted."

You and me both.

"Like I said, I don't go around kissing women like that. I don't know what came over me. But you and I—"

"Have a connection."

He nods, his half-grin growing into a smile. "We can't act this way around the men. I need this week to go well. I have so much riding on it."

"Trust me, I know what you mean. So do I." And he has no idea just how much I mean that.

"Good." He pulls his cap back down on his head and winks at me. My heart melts a few more degrees.

He climbs out of his seat and goes inside the building, leaving me alone to replay our kiss. A minute later, a large metal door rolls up, revealing countless tools lining the walls and an open concrete floor in the center. He returns to the side-by-side, as he calls it, and backs it into the building.

Such an odd name for a vehicle, since most cars require people to sit side by side. But he also calls ATVs four-wheelers, so maybe descriptive names are his thing. Huh. Wonder how he'd describe that kiss?

I have a few words of my own in mind, and they all mean "surprising." I'm surprised at how much I like kissing him, how good of a kisser he is, how kissing him brings me comfort and excitement at the same time. Most of all, surprised that he kissed me at all.

I have no clue as to Jack's dating life or lack thereof. If he dates much in Apple Cart or did before when he lived in Tuscaloosa. But I can almost bet he doesn't date people like me.

Which surprises me all the more that he initiated our first kiss.

He turns off the engine and gets out of the vehicle. I follow him, my eyes taking in a huge chain hanging from the ceiling.

"I've got to pack this deer for Macon. If you want, you can go back to the cabin and warm up a bit."

"Thanks. I think I'll make a cappuccino. Do you want one?" I've only seen him drink black coffee but want to share my honey vanilla cappuccino with him. I'd nearly fainted when I discovered a box hidden on a bottom shelf at Piggly Wiggly. Right between the off-brand cornflakes and powdered donuts.

He twists his mouth. Man, I want to kiss it.

"I'll give it a try." He laughs a little, the faint smile lines outlining his eyes.

I smile back and turn toward the open door. I walk to the lodge and enter through the back door. I shed my camouflage outerwear. Folding it neatly across one of the kitchen barstools, I retrieve the box of cappuccino. Maybe it will taste good. Jack has one of those old-fashioned coffee pots like in a fifties diner. A far cry from my stainless steel Keurig.

I boil the water and add the mix, then wait for it to steep. Two more days and a couple more meetings. That's all I've got to secure Macon and Ronald's business. I sigh. And to be with Jack.

I rest my elbows on the countertop and cradle my chin. I need to see this for what it is. Despite my attraction and chemistry with Jack, we could never have a relationship. Not with me in Atlanta and him out here in the sticks.

And neither of us are fit to move elsewhere. If he halfway cared for city living, he'd have stayed in Tuscaloosa. And if he thinks Tuscaloosa is too citified, he'll never make it in Buckhead.

The pot beeps, bringing me back to reality. I straighten and open a few cabinet doors until I find the antler-handled mugs. After filling each with cappuccino, I make my way back toward the building.

Jack said he needs to pack the deer. It shouldn't take too long to put a deer in a box, right? So perhaps we can sip cappuccino and watch the sunset together before the men return. And maybe Jack will find that romantic.

My face heats up at the thought of alone time with Jack. My stomach squirms. Not in a nauseous way but with anticipation.

But that anticipation transitions to nausea as soon as I enter the building. The blood drains from my face, and my jaw drops. I want to scream, but my throat catches.

When Jack said he needed to pack the deer, he didn't mention anything about mutilating it first. The poor thing hangs by its hind legs from the chain. It has been split down the middle, ribs showing where Jack has stripped away its fat.

"Bianca?" He stares at me with concern. As he comes toward me, and I lift my hands to give him a mug. My trembling fingers loosen, freeing both mugs. They shatter on the concrete, splattering my new boots with cappuccino.

Not knowing what to do next, I turn and run back to the lodge. And I don't stop until I make it all the way to my room.

After locking my door, I rush to the bathroom and wet a hand towel. Then, I furiously rub the toes of my boots before the sugary coffee concoction can dry.

As my hand rushes back and forth over the toe of my boot, my mind does the same over what I've just seen. Why would Jack do such a thing? Don't they have butchers for that? People with professional kitchen tools and hairnets? Not Jack with a pocketknife, dressed like someone walking out of a Waffle House.

I cringe and change into my lounging clothes. I stumble pulling on my pants as seeing all that blood made me woozy. I leave my boots by the sink to dry and hide under the bed covers. Maybe lying down will calm me.

How stupid am I to contemplate starting a relationship with a man so barbaric? How could I ever trust my heart to someone who willingly cuts out an animal's heart and tosses it in a bucket?

Perhaps this is for the best. Now I can talk myself down from my attraction to Jack and focus solely on the prize at hand. Proving my worth to Dad.

Jack

I stare at the puddle of tan liquid, flecked with chips of glass. Field dressing a deer isn't exactly appealing to most women, but I've never had one react like this.

Bianca's creamy skin faded white as bird poop sitting in the sunshine. I shake my head and toss an old rag on the ground to soak up the cappuccino. Then, I wander toward the edge of the shop in search of a broom. I don't want to chance tiny ceramic pieces pricking my dogs' paws later.

Counting both the time it took me to clean up Bianca's mess and the time it took me to contemplate what just happened, I'm now twenty minutes behind schedule.

I wash my hands in the corner sink and get back to work. Bianca freaking out like that proves how much she could never live in a place like Apple Cart or date a guy like me. I need someone who can walk up on deer guts without dropping things. Thank God she hadn't been holding a gun this time.

What was it with this woman and her butter fingers?

I continue cutting meat from the deer and sigh. What I really need is a steady income. Not a woman.

If I could go back in time a year, I wouldn't build that mansion of a lodge. At least not yet. I could've gotten a camper for me and let guests stay where I live now. Then, I could've slowly saved money to build the lodge without a mountain of debt.

But I have to admit that what sets me apart from other hunting camps is the lodge. A lot of the guests have my mindset of not caring where they sleep as long as it's in the dry. It's all about the hunt. However, I get business from many couples or out-of-towners who want the outdoors experience with a luxury feel. I can't offer that in my modest three-bedroom cabin with kitchen appliances older than me.

I fight this mental battle every month when the bills come rolling in. What can I do to bring in more money?

Why did I spend my life's savings on one huge house? And, worst of all, can I continue to keep up my business, or will I need to get a regular job to make up for losses? A job like I had before but hated.

I trim the last pieces of meat off Macon's deer and set down my knife. Admiring the stack of steaks, I toss the remaining meat into a bowl to be processed. That meat will make great sausage.

About the time it darkens outside, I hear the other side-by-side pulling up. I walk to the edge of the shop and see Macon and Ronald get out where we'd shot guns earlier. When Macon turns, I wave to get his attention. They climb back into the vehicle and drive toward me. Only when they make it close to the shop do I notice a deer hooked to the rack.

I motion for them to pull the vehicle into the shop, walking backward as they follow me. I hold up a hand when I get to the chain, and they stop a few feet away. "Wow, another big one."

"Yeah, he missed his buddy, so I put him out of his misery." Ronald laughs.

"You can leave it here, and I'll clean him, too. Unless you want me to take photos first."

"We took care of that already." Ronald taps his phone and hands it to me. His background image is a photo of him straddling the deer and pulling it up by the horns as if he won a bull fight.

"Indeed, you have." I snicker as he counts twelve prominent tines on the buck. "If either of you would like to donate some of meat for dinner, I can grill some farm-fresh steaks."

"Absolutely." Macon smiles.

Ronald strokes his chin, which has populated with gray whiskers since his arrival a few days ago. "How's about this.

Cook up some steaks from Macon's deer and mine. You make it where you know who's is what, and let's do one of those fancy taste-tests."

I laugh. "Challenge accepted."

The men hang around a little longer and examine the bust of Macon's deer, comparing it to what they could see of Ronald's hanging from the chain hoist. Then, Ronald mentions something about shooting darts, and they head back to the lodge.

I continue working on the deer, half-wishing they'd stuck around. With nobody talking to me, my mind drifts to Bianca. Her reaction to the deer fights her intense kisses for real estate in my brain.

Of all the women I've ever met, she intrigues me the most. So citified. But with a spark of something adventurous. When we first met and I pulled her from the mud, never in a million years would I have guessed she'd shoot a gun or go hunting.

Or kiss me.

I straighten my cap and select the steaks to grill tonight. Good thing Bianca has plenty of groceries for herself. There's no way I could convince her to eat deer after today.

I put away my tools and the meat I've wrapped from both deer. Then, I set the busts aside for the taxidermist to collect tomorrow. Each will make a nice trophy.

As I drive up to the lodge, lights shine from the game room window and from Bianca's bedroom. I enter a quiet kitchen and start preparing dinner. Baked potatoes, deer steaks, and a salad. Of course, I'll leave the meat off Bianca's plate.

Separating the steaks from the two deer offers me some amusement and keeps my mind off Bianca momentarily. But everything leads back to her in some way.

Once I take the steaks off the grill, I go find Macon and

Ronald. I've spent way too much time alone with my thoughts.

"Hey, Jack." Macon turns briefly when I step in the game room, then concentrates on the dart board again. He hooks his tongue over the corner of his top lip and throws the dart in the center of the board. "Ha ha."

Ronald downs half a bottle of Gatorade and slants his eyes at Macon as if challenging him to a duel. He steps forward and throws his dart. It sticks in the circle just outside of Macon's.

"Yes." Macon lifts his arms in victory. I chuckle. These guys sure do get animated when it comes to sporting competitions.

"Who's ready to see which deer tastes the best?" Both men head toward the door. Ringing a dinner bell wouldn't have grabbed their attention as much as saying that.

I follow them into the kitchen and pull down some plates. I get out forks, steak knives, and fixings for the potatoes as well. "Go ahead and help yourselves."

"You sure you know which steak came from which deer?" Ronald moves one steak around with his fork.

I nod. "Different plates, but I'm not telling whose is whose. Why don't you guys take a steak from each and remember which plate you took it from."

Ronald's face lights up. No wonder these guys have such a good business, as competitive as they are over silly things like darts and whose deer tastes the best.

I start to prepare my own plate but stop when I reach for a steak. Bianca needs to eat something, and I have no idea if she plans on coming down soon. I add extra salad to the plate and make a smaller plate with everything she might want to put on a baked potato. Then, I grab one of her apples from the counter.

"You guys go ahead. I'm going to see if Bianca wants

food." Macon mutters something in the form of a "thank you." Ronald already has a mouthful of steak. So I guess they're good.

I snatch a bottle of water, a few napkins and utensils, then head for the stairs. It takes only two steps for me to realize I don't have enough hands. The bottle of water squeezes from beneath my armpit and rolls down the staircase. I'll have to come back for it.

I adjust the rest of the items and walk with more caution this time. But I barely make it to the top without any casualties—the food and myself included.

I tiptoe to Bianca's door and set the food down, then hurry quietly back downstairs to retrieve her water.

It has rolled in front of my office doorway. I pick it up and face the office. What if I write her a note? Just a little something to check on her after what happened with the deer. That might be nice.

I step inside the office and find a note and pen.

Bianca,

Sorry about the deer this afternoon. I know it looked gross. Here is some food nobody had to slaughter to prepare.

Jack

I fold the note and head upstairs one last time. After placing the note by the plates, I start to walk away. But I want her to know there's food, especially since we finally have some things she'll eat.

Before I lose my nerve, I knock on her door.

CHAPTER EIGHT

Bianca

I settle into the sudsy water and inhale the aroma of my bubble bath. Now that the hunting is over, I can go back to smelling like roses—literally.

I'd called Dad earlier before shooting guns. So, I should have my mind on what he'd pointed out about Macon and Ronald's company. Instead, it's seesawing between Jack and that horror of a deer. My shoulders flinch as I sink them into the warm suds.

I close my eyes and fold a hot washcloth across them to try to relax. A few seconds later, a loud knock pounds on my door. I ignore it until the third knock. I sigh and fling the cloth to the floor. I stand, and suds crawl off my body to the water. I reach for my bathrobe a few feet away on a chair.

Apparently, it is a little farther than I thought. I have to stand on my toes and reach my arms long. "Just a minute." Maybe the person on the other side will hear that and stop.

I almost make it out of the tub when my toes slip, spilling me forward. Water sloshes on top of me. I lift onto my knees and blow a strand of damp hair from my eyes. I crawl toward the chair.

No sooner than I wrap the robe around myself, the door cracks. My fingers shake as I hurriedly tie my robe. The door opens wide while I'm still on the floor.

"Are you okay?"

It's Jack. Of course.

"Yes, I fell." I twist my mouth and glance at the balcony door. "Again."

"Let me help you up." He strolls over and takes one of my hands. He rests his other hand on my back.

I squeeze the robe with my free hand in case I didn't secure it enough. The tension of the moment mixed with the elation of Jack holding my hand makes me lightheaded. Once I'm halfway sure my robe won't fly open, I raise that hand to my temple.

"You're dizzy."

No kidding.

"Here." Keeping his hand on my back, Jack helps me into the chair and kneels beside it. "Sorry about knocking like that. I thought you might be out on the balcony."

I shake my head. "It's fine." I attempt to scold him for the interruption, but I then I look into his eyes. Those blue pools of concern wash away my worries about the dead deer.

"I brought you some supper."

"That's nice of you." As long as it doesn't include something from the meat market in your garage.

He stands and walks back to the door. He comes back with a huge plate of lettuce, the salad dressing I'd picked out earlier, and a zipper-sealed bag I'd prepped with salad toppings. He sets it on the desk and lifts his index finger as if telling me to wait.

I study the salad like it's a college exit exam. I don't want to wait. I'm starving, and in front of me is a delicious plate of Piggly Wiggly substitutes for my favorite salad.

Jack returns with a baked potato in foil and a plate full of toppings for it, plus a bottle of water and a note. "I didn't expect to come in."

I didn't expect you to, either.

"This note just says here's food and sorry about the deer." He stares down at the piece of paper, then sticks it on the desk by my food. "Like I said, I wasn't gonna come in, then I heard the crash."

My lips curve into a slight smile. I sense a pattern here. All I have to do anytime I want Jack is make a loud noise, whether screaming on a balcony or falling on hardwood floor.

"It's fine, Jack, I promise."

He nods and crosses his arms. "I don't want you thinking I'm some kinda barbarian since I skin deer."

A tiny laugh escapes my throat. That's exactly what I think. "I guess I didn't know what packing up a deer entailed."

He laughs nervously. "Where do you think we get all this deer meat I cook?"

I raise a shoulder. "Piggly Wiggly?"

Jack covers his eyes and laughs obnoxiously loud.

"What?" I straighten my shoulders and lift my chin. "You said yourself they sell local produce, so why not local meat?"

He rubs his jaw. "You do have a point. Maybe I need to talk to the butcher down there." Jack frowns at my salad, then meets my eyes. "So what did you think packing up a deer meant?"

"Oh," I sit back in my chair and sigh. "For some reason, I pictured Macon taking it home and having it stuffed. Like those big animals you see in sporting goods stores."

"Even if he wanted to stuff it, we'd need to clean out the innards first."

I wrinkle my forehead. "The what?"

"Innards. You know, the insides. But most people just mount the head and neck and eat all the meat."

The bacon bits setting next to my baked potato look less and less appealing the more he talks. Forget boycotting fried and fatty foods. After this trip, I may as well convert to veganism.

"I do it myself to save time for the hunters. That way, they can take their meat with them when they leave. And don't tell anyone around town I said so, but I'm as good a processor as any meat packing plant this side of the Mississippi River." He pushes his shoulders back and gives me a serious face.

I can't help but laugh at him bragging about cutting apart a deer. "Well, thanks for not putting any deer on my plate."

"Yeah, I didn't think now was a good time to try and persuade you to try it."

"No." I shake my head and laugh. He has a strange effect on me. A few hours ago, I wanted to run away from the deer destroyer, and now I'm glad he barged into my room to talk.

He peers out the window, then back at me. "I better go back down and eat with the guys. They've got a deer steak contest going on."

"What is that?"

"Ronald killed a buck before they came in for the day. So, I grilled up some steaks from each since they wanted to see which tasted best."

"Wouldn't they taste the same?"

Jack shrugged. "Depends. Some deer are more gamey than others. Of course, I cut away the fat from the steaks, which lowers the chances of that."

I swallow and slant my eyes toward the food. No way I'm eating those bacon bits.

"I'll leave you to it, then."

I sigh as he walks out and closes the door behind him. Despite the fact that he needs to entertain the guys and eat himself, and the more embarrassing fact that I'm wearing nothing more than a bathrobe and suds . . . I want him to stay.

⚝ ⚝

Jack

If I had more time and help, I might entertain the notion of opening a wild game cafe at the lodge. Macon and Ronald couldn't taste a difference in either of their steaks. Neither could I. All were cooked equally to perfection.

But I can't take people hunting, then cut and process their deer meat, and cook for an army. I'm not a pioneer woman.

Still, tonight's simple meal was a success. Macon and Ronald polished off all the steaks and didn't even leave room for grilled honeybuns. We chatted for a while after supper, and they shared hunting stories with me before going on to their rooms.

As soon as I finish cleaning the kitchen, I can head home to my own bed. I rinse the last pan and set it on a rack to dry, then reach for a towel and some disinfectant spray to clean the countertops. Thanks to not having any sisters—or siblings at all—Mom made sure I knew how to help clean.

"Ah, he cooks, and he cleans."

I jump, my elbow knocking the cleaning spray clear

across the counter. I didn't expect to hear from Bianca the rest of the night.

"And I field dress a mean deer." I cock the corner of my mouth into a smile as I turn to face her.

Blue flannel pajamas with pink flowers hang from her small body. Her blond hair is gathered in a mess on top of her head. She still isn't wearing any makeup. And she looks beautiful.

"I figured you'd gone to sleep by now." Mostly because I want to be asleep by now.

"I needed to get out of my room for a while. Been cooped up all afternoon."

I lift my chin and toss the cleaning rag on the counter behind me. "Your phone still working okay?"

"Yeah." Bianca's eyes wander around the room as if she's contemplating something, then they settled on me. "Jack, the more I replay it in my mind, the more I realize I was silly to overreact like I did about the deer."

I lift then drop one shoulder. "Nah, I get it."

"I broke your coffee mugs."

I laugh. "Those things needed to die."

Her remorseful glare disappears, and she bursts out laughing. "They were so ugly."

"So ugly." I laugh harder myself. We laugh together until Bianca starts snorting, which makes me laugh harder.

As we calm down, Bianca takes a deep breath as if she needs to reset her voice from laughing. "If you knew they were ugly, why did you buy them?"

"I didn't. They were a housewarming gift."

"From whom?"

I smile, then dip my head. "My mom." I slowly raise my eyes to Bianca covering her mouth and muffling a laugh. "Yeah. She said it would be a nice touch for my wilderness theme."

"And the fish mouth potholder?"

I grab the potholder from the drawer beside me and shove my hand into it. "This was all me." I open and close my hand, making the fish move its mouth. She doesn't even attempt to hide her laughter this time.

Once she gets her laughs out, she cranes her neck and stares at the deer antler chandelier above our heads. "I do like all these rustic-chic touches though."

"That would be my best friend's sister, Carolina. She's an interior designer."

"And a good one, I see." Her eyes drift to the arched doorway and back to the chandelier before returning to me.

I grin at her, then go back to wiping the countertops. "If you're hungry again, I can fix you a salad."

"No, I'm good, thanks." She steps closer. "Do you need any help?"

Boy, is that a loaded question. Can she snap her fingers and create a million minions to take care of everything I have to do, including a few to conjure up some extra cash? "No thanks. After I finish in here, I'm retreating to bed myself."

I read both pity and disbelief on her face. "Jack, you talked about expanding to do more with the lodge. Why don't you hire some help?"

Ah, the age-old answer everyone likes to give. If only it were an option.

I sling the cleaning rag across my shoulder and lean against the counter, crossing one foot over the other. "You know anyone who'd work for free? Because that's my budget." I run a hand through my hair and sigh. "My cousin comes out now and again to help with maintenance, and I buy a good bit of the food from Mrs. Mary's. But beyond that, it's all on me."

She frowns and comes over to lean beside me. "Maybe someone part time?"

"That's where Jonah comes in, when he's home from college. He gladly helps out since it was his grandparent's land, too. But all my money is tied up in this." I hold up my palms and glance around the massive kitchen.

"You just built this place, right?"

I nod. "We finished a little over a year ago."

"So, you got a construction loan?"

I nod bigger. "And I'm starting to regret that. I was so eager to open for business and do it right from the get-go. But now I think I should've built slowly and let the lodge pay for itself. Maybe let people stay at my place and I could've lived in a camper."

She places her hand on my forearm and gives it a few pats. I breathe deeply at her comforting touch. "This lodge is an impressive place, though."

"Exactly, and I don't foresee someone like you staying in a place like my old cabin from the 1960s."

She drops her hand and raises an eyebrow. "Someone like me?"

"No disrespect, but I don't imagine you stay in many small, outdated homes with two labs running around."

"I love dogs."

My eyes bug. "You do?"

"Yes, you shouldn't assume that because I don't enjoy watching a deer dressing or eating tons of meat that I hate animals."

She has a point. I had profiled her as someone who cared nothing about animals. "You're right, sorry."

"That's okay, I get it. But what I don't get is why you're afraid to expand your business."

I straighten and resume my cleaning ritual. How could someone who built a half-million-dollar home be called afraid to expand?

"Jack, don't get mad. I only meant that you have great ideas, and I'd like to see you succeed."

I toss the towel into the sink free-throw style and sit on a stool at the island. "Bianca, every penny I make goes toward my loan. I'm not afraid of expanding so much as I'm afraid to gamble on any of my ideas."

"I think hosting business meetings here was a great idea. Macon and Ronald are in their element, we all have great accommodations, and you're a very attentive host."

I smile. Well, I'm way more attentive to her than anyone else. "Thanks, it means a lot to hear you say that. I have a few more ideas, but if they don't do well, I'll have wasted my time and money."

Bianca pulls up the stool beside me and sits. "Like what?"

"I want to build a lake. That way, I can hold fishing tournaments and offer fishing in the hunting off-season. But it'll take a lot of my time."

"That sounds like a great idea. People could stay at the lodge and fish in the summer. And they could walk on the trails you use to get to the hunting fields, like the one I jogged on this morning."

"Yeah." I scratched my chin. "Oh, and I've been kinda thinking about making a shooting range."

"You mean the dirt pile?" Her nose scrunches.

"Yes and no. Like real targets. Metal, paper, fake deer. The possibilities are endless. I could do it in one of the empty fields and fence it off from the wildlife."

Bianca giggles.

"What?"

"It's cute how excited you got about that."

I shrug as my cheeks get hot. I stare at the ground a moment, then clear my throat. The excitement never lasts long, thanks to not having any extra money to invest in, well, anything.

"I mean it when I say I can't spare a dime, Bianca." I raise my face. Her green eyes are now full of concern. "I used my life's savings for a down payment. And Carolina did all the designing at cost. But to build something like this . . . It cost me a literal fortune. I know you deal with people like Macon and Ronald who probably live in something like this for their own homes. But I'm a first-generation college guy with a marketing degree. I've spent the last few years talking people into buying things they probably couldn't, or at least shouldn't, afford. Then, I got starry eyed and did the same myself."

Bianca reaches out and holds my hand. The smoothness of her skin glosses over my weathered knuckles. "Jack, I could help you with a business plan if you'd let me."

I sigh. "I don't need to unload my problems on you. I don't know why I told you all that." But I do know. Despite our differences, I like her. A lot. I trust her with business, and, just maybe, my heart. "I can't afford to pay you for your expertise."

The corners of her lips raise, and she gives my hand a gentle squeeze. "I think we can work something out." Then, she leans in and brushes her lips across mine.

I close my eyes for a split second, which is about how long the kiss lasts. Once my eyes are open, she has her back to me, walking away.

I can decipher the meaning behind a covered dish or a hint for an invitation to visit the baby deer at my place. But I'll never understand the games that city girls play.

CHAPTER NINE

Bianca

I blink as the sun dances through the tree branches outside my patio windows. I forgot to close the curtains last night. It's for the best, though, since I want to get in some exercise and make a smoothie before going over expansion plans with Ronald and Macon.

Last night gave me new insight into Jack. I never would've guessed he has so much financial pressure on him. And after staying here a few days and getting to know him on a much deeper level, I'm determined to find a way to help him make this place a go.

I change into leggings and a long-sleeved shirt. The view from my window indicates a beautiful day outside and a nice one for running. I lace up my shoes and make it to the door but freeze after turning the door handle. Do I really want to chance someone shooting at me while I run?

Dropping my hand from the door, I move back and

stretch. I read an article once about exercising while traveling. Of course, I always choose places to stay with full gyms and often a spa. Until now. Thanks, Dad. But the article did give a few tips for cardio I could put into practice.

I stretch my legs a little more before doing jumping jacks. Making a mental note to pack a jump rope next time interrupts my counting, so I move on to burpees. Ugh. Burpee should be a curse word.

After all the burpees I can physically stand, I jog in place to keep my heart rate high. I continue jogging in a small circle until I hear something behind me. I turn around to see my door half-open with Jack's face peeking through the crack. I scream and hop back from his view, knocking my knee on the bedpost. The door opens the rest of the way, and he comes in, holding a stack of towels.

As his eyes fall to my knee, he drops the towels and rushes to my side. "Are you okay?"

"Sure." I straighten my leg and hobble up onto the bed.

"What were you doing?"

I pull my knee to my chest and rub it with my palm. Meanwhile, my heart thumps a million miles an hour from the jogging . . . and from Jack.

"I was going to leave some fresh towels by your door, but it was half-open. I heard you scream, and then you fell into the bed."

I nonchalantly brush back some hair that has fallen from my ponytail. "I'm perfectly fine. Just trying to get in my morning cardio."

"Oh, I thought maybe you were trying to get warm."

"What?" I frown. Wouldn't I simply put on more clothes?

"You know. Like on those survival shows where they drop people off for dead in the middle of nowhere and they have nothing to keep them warm. So they just jog around."

I shake my head. "Never seen one of those."

"You're missing out."

I raise an eyebrow. I'm not so sure about that. Of all the drama reality TV had to offer, watching someone with nothing going on sounded like a big waste of my time.

He nods toward the balcony. "You know you're welcome to go running outside anytime."

I cross my arms. "Not worth the risk."

He laughs and shrugs. "Suit yourself." He crosses the room and bends over to collect the towels. My eyes drift toward his backside. I drop my head when he stands, embarrassed for having ogled him yet again. At least I wasn't walking this time.

I rub my knee as he brings the towels to my bed. He refolds a few, wafting an airy freshness my way. "There you go." He looks at my knee. "You sure you don't want a bag of ice?"

"Thanks, but I'll be fine. It's not nearly as sore as my head the other night." I clench my jaw, partly from my current pain and partly from the painful memory of smacking the glass door.

"Would you like some breakfast?"

I twist my mouth and give it some thought. "How about I cook for all of us."

"You . . . cook?" He looks skeptical of my suggestion.

"Yes, I can cook. Not deer, but, like, normal things."

He grins. "Oh, so deer isn't normal?"

"Not where I come from."

"Well, darlin', you're in Alabama now." He winks, sending a shiver down my back. Nobody has ever called me "darlin'" before. Or even "darling" with the "g" included. But I like that almost as much as I like him winking at me.

I grit my teeth as I straighten my leg, then stand. "Come on." I nod toward the door and head out. He follows on my heels. I limp a little down the stairs but fully recover by the time we reach the kitchen.

"I was going to just make a smoothie for myself, but I can cook some egg white omelets, too." I wash my hands and open the refrigerator.

"What's wrong with the egg yellows?"

"Hold this, please." I ignore Jack's yolk question and hand him the carton of eggs. Then, I bend back in front of the refrigerator. A minute later, my arms are so full of vegetables and cheese that I have to shut the refrigerator door with my foot.

"Wow. So is it because there won't be any room left for the yellow part?"

I roll my eyes. "No, it's healthier for your cholesterol to eat only the whites."

"With the amount of meat I ingest, I doubt an egg yolk will push me over."

"Suit yourself." I smirk, happy to throw Jack's rebuttal back at him. I locate the blender and start tossing in ingredients for my smoothie.

He scrunches his nose when I pour it in a glass. "That's not going in the omelet, is it?"

I laugh. "No, silly, it's my smoothie."

He puffs up his cheeks and widens his eyes. "You're gonna drink that?"

"I do at least three times a week."

"But it's the color of my tractor."

"That's because I have three healthy greens in it."

He grimaces, then opens the refrigerator. "Whatever. I'm cooking bacon."

I giggle at his reply, then swallow at a distant memory from my only long-term relationship. Cooking breakfast together was very much like playing house, which I'd done before with the wrong person at the wrong time. Not that Jack preparing bacon beside my omelet skillet meant anything like that. But it still reminded me of my past mistake.

I sigh and crack an egg in the pan. A moment later, Jack's hand touches my shoulder, startling me. "Look, it's cool if you want to drink the John Deere milkshake. I won't make fun anymore."

I turn my lips up best I can. "I'm not upset, just thinking."

He squeezes my shoulder, then removes his hand and sticks it in that hideous fish mitt. "What about?"

"A little about Outdoorsmen Oasis and a little about your business." I lie through my teeth, which is safer than the truth.

How do I tell my current love interest I'm thinking about the time I eloped with my high school boyfriend and my parents made us get an annulment? Oh, I don't.

I sprinkle cheese and sliced peppers and mushrooms onto my egg whites with a shaky hand. I've never admitted my failed marriage to anyone. And aside from my best friend and the people back home Rich told out of anger, nobody else knows about our marriage.

My dad bribed him not to leak anything to the press about Gerald Manderson's daughter's elopement. And, shallow as Rich is, that worked. But it only masked what had happened, not erased it. Now I'm stuck living with what-ifs.

What if I had heeded my parents' advice and focused on college before getting serious? What if I'd told my parents I wanted to marry Rich anyway? And what if he and I could've made it work?

That last "if" didn't come to mind often but resurfaced whenever I doubted my chances at a happily-ever-after. So, could that be why I'm thinking of it now, as I stand beside Jack?

"Man alive, I smell bacon." The deep voice coming from behind me interrupts my worries. I let out a laborious sigh, never so happy in my life to hear Ronald.

"Good morning, Ronald," Jack greets him.

I flip my omelet before turning around to say hello. Ronald greets me back.

"Macon up yet?"

Ronald cocks his head toward the back yard. "Yeah, he's about to shoot some before breakfast."

I look Jack in the eye and lift my shoulders high. "Would you imagine that. Someone shooting this early."

He slants his eyes and shakes a fish-mitted fist my way. I smile, satisfied with having proven my point.

"Ronald, I have some egg white omelets if you'd like to try one."

"Thanks, little lady, but I like my eggs like I like my women."

"Oh." I chew the inside of my jaw. I'm not sure I'm ready to hear his reason behind this.

"A little scrambled and not so flat."

And there it is. I fake a laugh. Ronald, nice as he is, has the same sense of humor as a clichéd crazy uncle.

Without saying a word, Jack cracks a few eggs into his bacon grease and starts scrambling away.

Macon comes in not long after we finish everything and surveys the spread of food. "Is that an omelet?"

"Yes." I beam. Finally, someone else around here who appreciates finer egg dining. "It's a vegetarian egg-white omelet."

"I see." Macon gives me a nervous smile, then passes over the plate of omelets for Jack's mountain of golden grease.

Jack winks at me and piles his own plate full of eggs and bacon. Then, he cuts a sliver of an omelet and slings it on top of his other food.

Maybe he will enjoy eating something lighter for a change. Even if it is marinating on a bed of bacon grease.

🦌🦌

Jack

Oatmeal cream pie and a bag of chips. Not an ideal lunch, but I have a lot of ground to cover while the guys and Bianca meet. Mrs. Mary brought by her vegetable soup and cornbread for them to eat, but I didn't have time to grab a bowl for myself.

I stop at the first feeder and check the varmint guard. And God bless America, it hasn't moved. I need to check the cameras to make sure coons haven't tried to eat there to know if it's actually working. I retrieve the SD chip from the camera and replace it with a fresh one. Once a week I change out the memory cards. It gives me a good excuse to watch what the cameras catch. Kinda like a coach watching game film.

The bin is about one-third full of corn, so I add more. Then, I drive the side-by-side to the next feeder and repeat the process. After covering all the feeder stations, I have long gone through both my snacks and a Mountain Dew.

As I cover the ground, I envision where I might build a lake and where I might set up a shooting range. Adrenaline rushes through my veins as I imagine families and other large groups enjoying different activities all year long. Only problem is, I can't set up shooting targets, help bait hooks, and lead hikes all at once. Either everyone will need to do the same activity at the same time, or I'll need to hire help.

And hiring help means money. I scratch the back of my

head and adjust my cap. It is the age-old question about the chicken or the egg. Which comes first? Hiring help for more activities or going ahead with activities to fund the help?

Unfortunately, what will make the best experience for guests won't make the best financial option for me.

I fight off the urge to park at the lodge and devour whatever is left of Mrs. Mary's soup. Instead, I drive home. I let Chocolate and Brownie outside, then fix a bottle for the baby deer. She's getting stronger by the day, thanks to her voracious eating.

"Come here, girl." I close the pen behind me and tiptoe toward the tiny deer. Once she sees the bottle, she heads my way.

I hold the bottle steady so she can suck on it, then stroke her soft head. "There you go, girl."

She butts her head a time or two but stops when I tilt the bottle higher. I might need to mix a bigger bottle tomorrow, since this one isn't lasting too long. She's come a long way from the day I found her alone in the woods.

Suction sounds echo from the empty bottle as she tries to get more. "I'll give you more tomorrow." I stroke her head once more before pulling the bottle away and strolling toward the fence.

I stare at the bottle as I walk, not lifting my head until I open the gate. That's when my eyes meet Bianca's. I jerk and take a step back.

She smiles. "Did I scare you?"

"A little bit." I return her smile.

She leans over the fence and looks behind me. "That was the sweetest thing I've ever seen in my life."

I turn toward the deer lying in a bed of hay, then back to Bianca. "You want to feed her?" It can't hurt to give her a bit more today. Besides, Bianca's reaction is well worth the gluttony.

Her eyes twinkle like jewels, and her mouth opens wide. "Could I?"

"Yeah. I can mix some more milk." I hold up the bottle. She hops a few times and claps her hands.

I shut the gate behind me and step past Bianca. "This way." I lead her to the shop. She halts at the entrance, her face growing pale.

"I keep the milk mix in here."

Frozen, she glares at the door. "Is the deer . . ."

I lift my eyebrows in question. She cups her hands around her throat and gags.

I laugh. "Goodness, no. As soon as I package the meat, I discard the carcass and get the bust to the taxidermist.

"Oh." She exhales and relaxes her shoulders.

I laugh again, thinking about what must've gone through her head when I led her here. I open the door, and we go inside.

Her eyes dart around the space before the fear fades from them. Maybe she doesn't trust me to tell the truth. I shake my head and snicker as I open the powder for the fawn's milk.

I add half the amount I used earlier, then go to the sink to add water.

"What's the deer's name?" She calls from behind me.

"The baby deer?"

"Yeah."

"Baby Deer."

"You haven't named it?" By her tone, you'd think it was a federal crime to not name an orphaned deer I fully intend on turning back into the wild to kill.

"Nope."

"How long have you been feeding it?"

I glance up at the rafters and try to remember when I found her. "Uh, like three weeks." I look back at Bianca.

Her jaw drops. "How could you feed something so precious for three weeks and not give it a name?"

I shrug.

"We've got to name that sweet baby." Her eyes plead with me.

"Okay." I shake the bottle and start back toward the deer pen.

"Is it a girl or boy?"

"A girl."

"Awwww." She clasps her hands together and holds them under her chin. "How precious."

If I had known she'd react like this, I'd have taken her straight from the mud to the deer pen, day one. I open the gate and wait for her to go in. Then, I follow and shut it.

The deer hasn't moved from the hay, but wobbles to her feet when she spots the bottle. She prances over to us, white tail wagging.

I hand Bianca the bottle. She braces both hands on it. "What do I do?"

"Just hold it steady. She knows what to do."

Her face lights up as the deer nudges the bottle. "Look, she has tiny white spots all over her face. Let's name her Freckles."

Why not? It sounds more original than Baby Deer. Not that it matters to Baby Deer, as long as she gets her milk.

"You can pet her, too."

Bianca smiles wider as she lets one hand move from the bottle to the deer's nose. The deer flinches, causing Bianca to toss the bottle. Milk spews over our heads and falls in droplets onto her fleece sweatshirt. "Oh, no."

I laugh and retrieve the bottle. "You're doing fine, but you can't loosen your grip. This baby deer is stronger than she looks."

"You mean *Freckles* is stronger than she looks." She

smirks while pinching the bottom of her fleece and fanning the milk off. Some of the drops fall, and others soak in. When she gives up trying to clean it off, I hand her the bottle.

"Thanks." She wrinkles her forehead as she grips the bottle tightly with her right hand. She rests her other hand on Freckles' nose when the deer steps up to the bottle.

The strain of concentration on Bianca's face as she white-knuckles the bottle is adorable. Soon the air-sucking sound returns, and I put my hand on the bottle to pull it away. Her hand lingers on mine as she hands over the bottle.

"You did it."

"I've never done anything like that before." She throws her arms around my neck. I daydream for a second about how nice it would be to have her here all the time. Helping with the deer, offering ideas to broaden my menu options.

I want to kiss her, but I can see Ronald and Macon in the distance. I drop my arms and clear my throat. She turns around and notices them. "Oh."

"I'd better get back to the lodge anyway. Do you want a ride?"

"Sure."

She follows me to the side-by-side and gets in. I toss the bottle in the back for now.

Chocolate waddles around a few yards from us. "Oh, wait. I need to put my dogs in the house first."

"The labs you mentioned?"

"Yeah."

Bianca smiles.

I drive to my house and call the dogs. They wag over to me. "Meet Chocolate and Brownie."

Bianca leans over and says hello to them in a kidlike voice.

"It won't take but a second." I get out, collect the empty

milk bottle, and lead the dogs up the porch and inside. I set the bottle in the sink and pet both of the dogs. Before going back out, I grab a couple of treats and toss them in their dog beds. They trot over and start chowing down.

I open the front door to Bianca. "Is this where you live?"

"Yeah, it was my grandparents' place before." I palm the back of my neck and glance back at my living area. There was a reason I hired Carolina to decorate the lodge.

Wallpaper older than me lines the kitchen walls, offset by ugly linoleum that bleeds into fuzzy brown carpet. If I had to give this house a theme, I'd call it 1970s bachelor pad.

Bianca doesn't say a word, just scans the area as she had the shop. A slight grin rests on her face. "I really just wanted to be alone so I could kiss you."

"Oh, you did?" My face pulls into a smile.

She nods. "I could tell you wanted to kiss me out there, but not with the guys close."

"Is that so?" I go plop down on the couch. Chocolate joins me.

Bianca crosses her arms and raises an eyebrow before coming to sit by me. I run a hand down her face, landing it on her cheek. I move toward her and close my eyes. Her smooth lips melt into me as I wrap an arm around her waist and kiss her deeper.

We continue kissing until something wet sweeps across my jaw. I flinch, confused at how Bianca could kiss me and lick my face all at the same time. Then, she pushes back, so I open my eyes. Chocolate is within an inch of my face, her sloppy tongue wagging. She sniffs the air, then licks me from my chin to my forehead.

Bianca squeals with laughter. I pull the bottom of my shirt up and wipe the dog slobber from my face.

"Well, that's the first time I've ever had two girls kiss me at once."

CHAPTER TEN

Bianca

I pat the dog's head and laugh. I like dogs but don't care for their kisses. Jack tugs at the dog's collar, so that she jumps off the couch.

"Bye, Brownie." I stroke her black tail as she hops down.

"No, that's Chocolate." He nods toward the kitchen. "Brownie is in there."

I scrunch my forehead. "So Chocolate is not the chocolate lab?"

"No."

"Huh." Yet more proof that he isn't skilled at handing out pet names.

He smirks. "Come on. I need to get back to the lodge. The guys are probably ready to hunt."

We step onto the porch, and he shuts the squeaky screen door behind us. I now understand why he built the lodge.

This cabin works fine for a single man, but it doesn't give off rustic retreat vibes like the lodge.

I stare at my milk-soiled pullover as we drive the short distance to the lodge. I half-regret not buying one of those dowdy unisex coats at the coffin place. It would've been a smart investment, considering what I'll have to spend on dry cleaning once I get home.

Home. I suck in a deep breath. Thanks to Jack's help, I've learned to relate to Macon and Ronald and drawn a solid business plan to please them. Also thanks to Jack, I've developed feelings I forgot existed.

But tomorrow I'll leave all this behind: the outdoors, Alabama, and Jack.

I admire his profile. Why can't a guy this handsome and caring and skilled live in Atlanta? Saying goodbye won't be easy. Maybe I can tie him up with that chain hanging in his metal building to kidnap him. Of course, kidnapping is hard to do when your only transportation is a ride-share.

We park by the back porch, where Ronald and Macon sit talking.

"Deer feeders are all stocked, and cameras are loaded." Jack hops out of the vehicle and shoves his hands in his pockets. "And Bianca bottle-fed Freckles."

The corners of my lips lift with pride. Aside from pet-sitting a friend's Maltipoo in college, I've never helped take care of an animal before.

"Who's Freckles?" Macon moves his eyes between Jack and me.

"Binaca named the deer." The tone of Jack's voice lets me know he still doesn't think giving Freckles a name was necessary.

"Speaking of freckles, I need to go change." I grimace at the flecks of milk soaked into my fleece.

"Why don't you go hunting with us?" Ronald calls from behind as I start toward the house.

I halt and turn my head. "I'm wearing perfume and makeup."

Ronald shrugs. "We're in no hurry."

I muster a slight smile. "Give me thirty minutes?"

The men nod in unison, then continue talking. I go inside and make my way up the towering stairs to my room. I still have the scentless shampoo and soap, compliments of Jack's stash.

I lock the bedroom door behind me and begin to undress. A sour milk smell drifts to my nostrils as I pull the fleece over my head. Gross. I toss it aside with my other garments that need a good cleaning.

Time to de-scent myself once again. I step into the stone-walled shower and lean my head back, letting the warm water make a mess of my makeup. As mascara trickles down my cheeks, I remember Jack mentioning scent-free makeup.

I hurriedly wash myself with Jack's odor-free supplies and reach for a towel. With one hand, I blow-dry my hair. With the other, I search online for unscented makeup. It is a thing. Some brands brag that their products are designed for highly sensitive skin. I scroll down and find two different makeup brands promoting makeup for female hunters.

I almost drop my phone with excitement while I click on the first result for hunting makeup. As soon as I dry my hair and put on clothes, I bolt downstairs.

I make it to the kitchen to find the camouflage romper thingy I wore earlier folded on the countertop. I clumsily step into it, not bothering to take off my boots, and walk outside as I zip it.

"Macon, Ronald." I smile when they turn their attention to me. "I've got a product great for your store."

I hand my phone to Macon. He holds it out a few inches

and enlarges the screen view. "Hmm. Scentless makeup. I saw something like this once at a trade show."

"I would so buy this."

Ronald steps behind Macon and looks at the screen. "Yeah, I told Macon it was a waste of shelf space. No woman who hunts cares for going without makeup."

"But women who do care to wear makeup might be more inclined to hunt with their husbands if they could keep it on."

Macon lifts his eyes. "That's a good point. I've never thought of it that way."

"Good marketing, Miss Manderson." Jack winks at me.

My cheeks flush as I pull my hair back into a hair tie. Macon hands back my phone and smiles. I sway, silently celebrating my brilliant idea. Then, I follow the men as they file into the vehicles.

Ronald slides into the passenger seat by Macon and smirks at me. My stomach churns a bit. Is that his subtle approval of me being with Jack? I drop my gaze and step into Jack's side-by-side.

"We need to let you kill a deer today," he says as soon as I sit.

I exhale and squint my eyes to try to combat a sudden headache. "Uh, you do realize I first touched a gun yesterday."

"Yeah, and you did pretty well."

I fix my eyes on the trees we pass. Could I actually shoot a live animal? That had to be much harder than a hitting a big red circle on a pile of dirt.

Jack says nothing else until we pull up to the treehouse. "All right, we'll take everything up, then I can walk you up, if you want."

I nod. Sitting somewhere high doesn't bother me. It's the way up that makes me nervous. I busy myself by flicking the zipper on my camouflage outerwear while the guys carry water and guns up the ladder. When Jack returns alone, I get out and meet him at the steps.

"Okay." I step on the bottom rung and turn my head.

"I'm right behind you."

My lips curve with the assurance that he'll catch me if I fall again. A minute later, I make it to the top and fling my arms over the floor. Sweat beads behind my ears as I heave myself up into the house. Whew. The scary part is over.

Jack slides in behind me, making my extreme effort laughable. He goes to the camera bag and sets up everything as he had the day before.

Deja vu sets in when I sit beside Macon and peer out the opening. But it quickly disappears when Jack hands me a gun. My hand shakes as I hold it against the wall.

"You can do this. We'll help you." Jack's eyes move from my face to Macon and Ronald, who nod in agreement.

Jack helps steady the gun in front of me. Then, I shift back in my chair and try not to worry about it propped between my legs.

A half-hour passes, according to my phone. According to my nerves, a day passes. As Ronald whispers something snarky about Macon's gun being inferior to his, a deer prances into the clearing.

A big deer.

Everyone goes silent. I straighten in my chair, wiggling the cushion beneath me. I lean my head toward the window opening. Jack reaches for my gun and whispers in my ear, "This is your deer."

I wring my hands while Jack clicks a few things on the gun and looks through the magnifying glass circle on top. Then, he hands it to me and circles behind me. "Hold up the gun and look in the scope."

Oh, yeah, that's what the magnifying circle is called. I

breathe in through my nose, afraid breathing through my mouth might shake the gun. Then, I wink and center the tiny lines to the deer.

"Once you've got it, pull the trigger."

I close both eyes and pull the cold metal with my index finger. Ronald shouts something obscene, and applause rings out around me. I open my eyes to a fallen deer.

I move my head away from the gun, and Jack takes it from me. I stare down at the deer—my deer—and blink a few times to make sure my eyes don't deceive me. "I can't believe I did that." I killed a real live deer . . . with my eyes closed!

"You did great." Macon lifts his hand for me to high-five. I slap his hand and grin.

Jack stands. "Let's go down and look at it." He sticks his head out of the hut and makes it down the ladder in two steps. I fight the urge to roll my eyes at how easily he gets down.

I sit at the edge of the platform and stick one foot two rungs down, then inch my way to the bottom, all the while facing the ground in front of me. Jack stays close by, which somewhat eases my fear.

We walk to the deer and kneel down. I stroke its face in a moment of remorse. "He's so pretty. I feel bad about killing him."

Jack puts a hand on my shoulder. "He's a wild animal, and one we eat. It's not like you shot Chocolate or Brownie."

I moan with terror. My stomach churns at the idea of shooting a dog. Jack sure got the point across on that one.

"Let me take your picture with it." He stands and backs up a few feet, retrieving his phone from his front pocket.

I position myself beside the deer as I saw Macon do yesterday. Then, I grab the horns and tug the head. It's much heavier than it looks, but I manage to lift it a few inches. "Like this?"

"Perfect." Jack smiles and snaps photos, as if he's a proud parent taking first day of school pictures.

He snaps more photos than I can count, then puts his phone away and backs the side-by-side up to the deer. A minute later, Macon emerges from the hut and helps him position the deer on the vehicle.

"Okay, Bianca." Jack slaps his hands together. "You ready to take this ten-pointer to the lodge?"

I nod, glancing at the horns. I count ten spiky points. Only a few less than Macon's deer the day before. I climb into the side-by-side and hold onto my favorite handle. Jack gets in and cranks the engine as Macon returns to the shooting house.

As we ride back, I rest my head against the seat, satisfaction plastered across my face. Never in my lifetime would I have thought myself capable of killing a deer. Physically or mentally. Just a week ago, I wouldn't have set foot in a hunting shack. Much less clad in faded camouflage.

Jack parks beside the metal building where the massacre occurred yesterday. My stomach burns as I recall the crime scene. He would do the same in a minute to my majestic creature.

"Don't worry, I won't start on the deer until you're gone."

My shoulders relax. He read my mind.

"I want to take a few more pictures."

I laugh. "You're worse than my mother."

Jack wraps an arm around me and pulls me close for a selfie. I beam. We look good together, even though I'm not fixed up properly.

"Well, a first kill is a big accomplishment. A rite of passage, if you will." He smiles, then glances back at the deer.

"You know, it's customary to put a little blood on your face from the first deer you kill."

"Eww." I grimace at the idea of blood on my face.

"Only if you want to, but it would make for a memorable photo." His clear blue eyes dance with excitement as he peers into my eyes. Into my soul.

"Why not?" The question was more for me than Jack, but he jumps out of the vehicle as soon as I ask.

I sit still as he dabs blood on both my cheeks with his soiled fingers. The weirdest makeover I've had by far. An iron smell drifts up my nose, making me a little nauseated. But Jack grins and smooths my cheeks with his thumb.

Then, he closes the space between us and presses his mouth into mine. I wrap my arms around his neck and forget about everything else. Even having yucky animal blood on my face.

Jack

I lean my forehead against Bianca's and smile. Every time we kiss, I want to tell her how much she means to me. But she'll go back to Atlanta tomorrow, back to city life where she wears tight skirts instead of camo coveralls and highly scented makeup instead of stinky deer blood.

I stand and laugh at her smudged face. "Why don't you stand by the deer one more time since you have the blood on your face? I'll take a picture."

She gives me an apprehensive smirk but gets out and does it anyway. I hold my phone in front of her. "Say cheese."

She rolls her eyes and giggles before showing off her perfect teeth. I snap a few photos, including one of her rolling her eyes, then show them to her.

"Eww, my face is a mess."

"Yeah, sorry. I might've had something to do with that." I wink. I was to blame for both dousing her face with deer blood and smearing it during the kiss.

"Well, you've got some on you, too." She reaches out and wipes my cheek with her thumb.

I turn the phone to selfie mode and use the camera as a mirror. "Yep, caught red-handed . . . or red-faced. I'd better go remove the evidence." I have the redneck equivalent of lipstick stains, and I wear it proudly.

She laughs.

"Let's back the deer in." I get back in the side-by-side and notice her hanging back. "I promise, we're just parking it."

She nods and gets in. "Good."

I back up to the shed, then open the large, rolling garage door. I continue backing inside and park by the chain I use to hang deer for cleaning.

"I think I'm going to take a bath and remove any evidence."

"Okay." I smile as she climbs out and heads toward the lodge. Her hair sways when she walks, and her cute figure is dwarfed by my bulky coveralls. I silently pray for the weatherman to call a snow warning in the hope that she won't be able to fly out tomorrow.

I watch her walk away until her blond hair fades against the dry winter grass, then I focus on the dead deer. I grab the chain, prepared to tie its hind legs when my stomach aches. Weird, but I want to keep the deer as a memento of her first kill and her time here with me.

I let go of the chain and stare at the deer. What if? I reach for my phone and pull up the number for my taxidermist. If

I can't keep Bianca here, I can at least keep her deer. Pathetic as that sounds, it lifts my mood.

After arranging for Roy to come pick up the deer, I drive across the shop and roll the deer onto a wooden trunk against the far wall. That will free up the side-by-side for use while I wait on Roy to collect the deer.

I notice a smudge of blood on my hands and remember my face. I walk to the sink and wet a paper towel to wipe off the blood. Then, I check my appearance in the dingy mirror hanging above the sink. I wipe the back of my arm across my face, letting my sleeve soak up any remaining water. I toss the paper towel in the trash and stick my hands in my pockets. If I don't have to clean a deer, I can go home and take a shower before dinner.

That plan falls through as I meet Ronald and Macon driving up with a whopper of a deer on the back of their side-by-side.

"Another one bites the dust." Ronald beams. "Thirteen pointer, baby. I knew I could catch up to Macon."

I laugh. Their competitiveness amuses me. It's offered quite the entertainment this week. "Let me open the door, and you can back it up to the chain I have hanging inside."

"All right." Macon clicks the side-by-side into reverse as I go back inside and unhinge the door. At least I would just be cleaning one deer as previously planned, not two.

I stand by the chain and lift a hand to motion for Macon to keep backing up, then straighten my palm when the vehicle reaches the chain.

The men get out and hover over the deer, debating whether it's tines are as long as those on the deer from yesterday. Of course, Ronald tries to convince everyone this was by far the biggest kill of the week. I can't argue with his confidence. No wonder he does so well in business.

They chat a few more minutes as I secure the deer's hind

legs to the chain. Then, they step back and watch as I hoist it into the air. Ronald admires it another minute, pointing out all the best features of his kill.

"You're such an excellent hunter, but I can beat you any day in a game of pool." Macon crosses his arms and stares down his friend.

"You're on." Ronald slaps Macon's shoulder before marching out of the shop. Macon follows him toward the lodge, leaving me alone to dress the deer.

I check my phone. I'd best get to work before Mrs. Mary comes by to help cook. Lately, I've made a habit of hiring her to come cook on site for a guest's last night. That frees me to mingle with everyone and offer everyone a top-notch meal, which I hope will undo any negative memories they have about the food I've made.

I clean my best knife and examine the deer. Ronald might not have exaggerated as much as usual. This thing is a beast.

As I chip away at getting all the best cuts of meat, my mind drifts back to Bianca killing her first deer. Little did she know how much it attracted me to see her in head-to-toe camo with blood on her cheeks. Not that the tight skirts didn't do the trick. But seeing her today gave me a sliver of hope she might want to start a relationship with a country boy.

I shake my head and get back to work. I have a lot of meat to pack, and the sun has set behind the trees. Mrs. Mary might already be at the lodge, but she knows what to do.

The meat grinder starts to hum, breaking the silence. I blow into my hands as a cool breeze sweeps through the shop. Maybe God's answering my snow prayer.

I finish grinding the sausage and seal it beside the vacuum-packed steaks. I put the meat in a Styrofoam cooler and label it with the date and Ronald's name. Then, I place that in one of my deep freezers against the wall. Between this deer and what's left from yesterday's, Ronald will eat good for a few weeks.

Once I clean the area and put away my tools, I close the doors and drive to the lodge. I enter through the back patio door to Mrs. Mary humming in the kitchen.

"Hi, Mrs. Mary."

"Hey there, sugar." She smiles, revealing the slight gap between her two front teeth. She pours some white powder into a pot and stirs it.

"What's that?" I hope it's the beginning of a cake. Or cornbread, since there wasn't any left when got back yesterday.

"I can't tell you my secrets."

"Okay." I raise my palms in surrender before rolling up my sleeves and turning on the faucet. "Need any help?" The warm water soothes my cold hands.

"I'm good. Why don't you go take a shower and entertain that pretty little thang in there."

I cut off the water and frown. "I always entertain *all* the guests."

"Mmm hmm." Mrs. Mary laughs when I face her. "Jack Jackson, I've known you your whole life. And I know when you're sweet on somebody."

"Is that so?" I cock my head and cross my arms.

"Yes, sir. And you've fallen for this girl."

She's on to me. I sigh.

"What's the matter, sugar? She not feel the same way?"

I uncross my arms and lean back on the counter. "She likes me too, but . . ."

"Then what's there to but about?" She breads some pork chops, causing my stomach to growl with anticipation.

"She's going back to Atlanta tomorrow."

"And?"

"I live in rural Alabama, hours away from her." I remove my cap and run a hand through my hair. "And this can't compare to her high-powered career and shopping and restaurants and all that in the city."

"How do you know that?" She turns her head and gives me a scolding glare.

I clench my jaw and inhale a huge puff of air. I let it out and place my cap back on my head. "I just think . . ."

"You think. But do you know what *she* thinks?"

I shrug. She makes a great point. If I want to pursue a relationship with Bianca, I need to express the seriousness of my feelings toward her. And I have to do it before she leaves.

But what if she doesn't feel the same way?

CHAPTER ELEVEN

Bianca

I sip my water and laugh at Macon and Ronald's banter. Their commonality ends with hunting and outdoors. But they complement one another well, and I've enjoyed working with them this week. As much as I hate to admit it, my dad was right. There are a lot of successful, smart people in the world who I'll miss out on meeting if I keep to my preferred clientele.

A week ago, I was up to my armpits in massage oil at a New York City spa. If not for Dad's ultimatum, I would've never considered having a gun in my armpit. Much less doing so in the middle of a quiet forest with a bunch of guys.

"Mrs. Mary, these potatoes are delicious. What did you put in them?"

"I'm afraid that's a secret, sugar." She smiles widely before taking a bite of bread.

I had heard someone in the kitchen and expected Jack

but met Mary instead. We talked a while before Macon and Ronald migrated toward the noise after their battles in the game room. By the time Jack made it back to the lodge, Macon had invited Mary to stay and eat.

"It's all delicious." Macon adds his opinion as if eating two pork chops hasn't shown his approval.

"Thank you all. I enjoy cooking more than just about anything."

"Yes, everyone, enjoy. It's back to deer poppers tomorrow." Jack raises his glass of sweet tea and smirks.

"Nothing wrong with that. Nothing at all." Ronald never misses a chance to sing his praises for deer poppers.

"I can bring you guys by some pie depending what time you're leaving."

"I'll stay for pie." Macon grins.

"I can drop some off after my lunchtime rush." Mary settles back in her chair, satisfaction on her face.

Seeing people content with what they do for a living is one of the reasons I enjoy working with entrepreneurs. And one of the many reasons I want to help Jack. His face glows every time he goes hunting or talks about it.

In a perfect world, I'd tie him with that heavy chain and drag him back to Atlanta. But he needs as much freedom as the animals roaming his property, if not more.

I sigh and pick at my vegetables. I've come to care a lot for Jack over the past few days, even before we kissed. And those emotions intensify with every moment we spend together. I'll miss him like crazy after tomorrow.

The chatter among everyone else muffles to mush as my head fills with memories of the first time I laid eyes on Jack. His scruffy face, homely attire, and the most gorgeous eyes I've ever seen.

Those eyes. I observe his face from across the table, my own face warming when he meets my gaze. He winks, drawing my mouth into an instant grin. Maybe nobody notices this exchange between us. But even so, I no longer care. My time with him is limited.

My phone vibrates against the wooden table, bringing me back to the reality of my surroundings. I pick it up and read "Dad" on the screen.

"Excuse me." I leave the table and make my way to the edge of the patio where my phone magically grows three bars of service. Random, but great.

I click on the missed call and hug my chest as I wait for him to answer. It has gotten a lot colder since I walked from the garage in Jack's camouflage overclothes.

"Hi, Dad."

He wastes no time asking me about the business plan. I fill him in on some of the key points for Outdoorsmen Oasis. Excitement rings out in his voice as he praises me for my great ideas and for connecting with the clients. I relax, no longer worried about the crisp air.

As he continues to sing my praises, he says something I don't want to hear. That I am just like him.

Am I?

The chill from before has returned. This time, it goes beyond skin deep. My bones freeze while he declares how I am his spitting image. In a business sense, that is fine. More than fine. Great. Even if he is such a workaholic that he has never engaged in any recreational activities he couldn't count as a tax deduction.

But on a personal level . . . whether he meant "just like me" to encompass all of his attributes, that's how I took it. And I don't care to end up married three times. I shudder. Thanks to Rich, I'm already headed in that direction.

"Are you still there?"

I hold the phone out and wince. My dad may as well be

on speaker phone. But maybe he needed to yell to get my attention.

"Oh, yes, Dad." I sigh and try to stop imagining myself as a female version of Gerald Manderson. "Can I speak to Mom?" May as well change the subject before I get nauseated over my future.

"No, she's on a trip."

"Where to now?" Once I'd moved out for good, Mom started traveling more. It began with a weekend trip once a month and slowly morphed into staying gone more than she stayed at home.

"When was she last home?" I clutch my phone tightly, almost afraid to hear his answer. And for good reason.

Apparently, Janet Manderson hasn't spent a night at home all month. I breathe in the cool air and hold it. When I open my mouth to speak, nothing comes out. My mom calls all the time from her cell phone. It's never occurred to me to take note of where she is each time.

Once my voice returns, I tell Dad goodnight and hang up the phone. I drop to the ground, not caring about the cold from the stone patio seeping through my jeans.

I'd met Mom for lunch twice this month, plus I recalled her saying she was shopping in Buckhead during one of our phone calls. So why would she not have come home for a solid three weeks? Better yet, if she wasn't going home, where was she going?

I swallow back vomit and run my hands up and down my cold thighs. None of this could mean good news for my parents' relationship. And even though I was a grown woman on my own, it didn't hurt any less.

After the initial shock wears off, I slowly stand and compose myself for going back inside. Not that this should come as a surprise. The more I recount the past few years, it all points to problems between my parents.

Too bad I've been too self-absorbed to notice.

I open the back door to Jack rummaging through the freezer. He lifts his head when the door shuts. "Hey, you look cold."

I nod and force a closed-mouth smile. No sense in letting my parental problems leak onto everyone else.

He straightens with a tub of Blue Bell ice cream in his hands. "I guess you won't want any dessert until you warm up, then."

I shrug. Sweets are my weakness whenever I have a bad day. "Do you have honey buns?"

He narrows his eyes toward the pantry door. "I can in five minutes."

I laugh. My heart warms knowing he can cheer me up no matter what.

"Why don't you let everyone know I'm grilling honey buns." He wiggles his eyebrows and opens the pantry door.

"Okay." I pass by, squeezing his arm as I do.

How long has it been since I've seen my parents' touch? No matter a kiss, but simply an affectionate touch. Or even seen them together?

I flutter my eyelids and swallow back a tear as I cross the hallway to the dining room. I lift my eyes to an empty room. I breathe in and out a few times before going to find everyone. I follow the sound of voices and find everyone congregated in the main living area, with Mary standing near the door.

"There you are, sugar. I wanted to say goodnight before I leave."

I smile and hold out a hand. "It was a pleasure to meet you, Mrs. Mary."

She shakes my hand, then pulls me in for a quick hug.

"Same here. Don't be a stranger, now. Come by the diner next time you visit, and I'll fix you up something good."

"I bet. Thanks for the invitation." I smile at the idea of eating in a quaint Alabama diner full of Mrs. Mary meals. The perfect setting for a lunch date with Jack.

Mary waves to the men as she leaves, closing the door behind her. A cool whoosh of air rolls in as the door shuts, hitting me in the face and shattering my daydream. A lunch date with Jack? When exactly was that supposed to happen? It wasn't like I could commute three hours for a chef salad.

I rub my forehead, then walk away from the door. Ronald and Macon are watching one of those reality TV shows about man jobs.

"Jack wanted me to tell you he's grilling honey buns."

"Best news since my last deer." Ronald unglues his eyes from the screen long enough to smile back at me.

"I'll let you know when they're ready." I nod and back out of the room. I go sit on a stool in front of the kitchen island. The fur agrees with jeans much more than yoga pants.

My eyes drift toward the deer antler chandelier. Aside from one steakhouse in Atlanta, I've never seen another place with these. I'll miss all the rustic touches of the lodge. Especially its rugged owner.

I rest my head in my hands and stare at the stone surface in front of me. Jack can't lose this place or his business. If it transforms half its guests the way it has me . . .

I wouldn't call myself an outdoors enthusiast by far. But considering that I entered this world in stiletto boots and morphed into a camouflage-clad, gun-shooting woman who doesn't have to wear makeup. That's quite the transformation.

The subtle pattern in the stone swirls out of focus as I brainstorm ideas for how I can help Jack's business. Cold hits my back, causing me to blink. I turn around to Jack coming inside with a pan of honey buns.

Yeah, I'll need to jog in place again tonight.

I lick my lips, anticipating the warm gooeyness. "I'll go let the guys know they're ready. Ronald was pretty excited about them."

He smiles. "I'm sure."

Gosh, how I'll miss that smile. I don't even mind that his five-o'clock shadow has returned. Perhaps he only shaves for church.

I stand in the living area entryway a minute, baffled by the men on TV. Who in their right mind would take to the ocean in a tiny rowboat at night during a thunderstorm? But I can see how it makes for solid entertainment. It's sucked Ronald and Macon to the screen.

"Honeybuns are ready." And just like that, their eyes leave the screen. I giggle as Macon pauses the show, and they immediately spring to their feet.

The honey scent has taken over the kitchen by the time we make it to the doorway. Jack busies himself scooping ice cream on top of the snack cakes.

Ronald grabs the first bowl and looks at Jack. "Is it all right to eat in the living room?"

"Sure." Jack shrugs as if nobody has ever asked him that before.

Macon thanks Jack for making honeybuns again and joins his friend. A few seconds later, the TV echoes in the background. I settle onto a stool, happy to have some alone time with Jack that doesn't require sneaking away from the guys. Between honeybuns and deep-sea fishing in a storm, they have plenty to occupy themselves.

I've guarded myself around Jack ever since Ronald walked up on our first kiss. Of course, at that point the business deal was in play, and everyone here is an adult. But I don't want anyone getting the impression that I go around kissing guys everywhere. Because that isn't the case at all.

Jack sticks a spoon in my bowl and straddles the stool beside me. He pulls the last bowl in front of him and raises a heaping spoonful of dessert to his mouth.

My eyes grow glossy as I study Jack. Now is as good a time as any to let him know my plan.

"Jack?"

"Hmm." He rubs his lips together and swallows the dessert puffing up his cheeks.

I smile and wipe a drip of ice cream from the corner of his mouth. "I believe I've come up with a way you can pay off the lodge."

He raises his eyebrows. "Ah, the Georgia lottery. Could you pick me up some scratchers on your way home?"

I laugh, then massage my forehead. "As much as I adore your sarcasm, this has nothing to do with chance."

"Then, please, do tell." He pushes his almost-empty bowl aside and leans closer. "I'm all ears."

"Okay." I squirm on my stool with excitement. "I've been checking locations around the southeast for Macon and Ronald to start new chains. We've thrown around a few options in Alabama, but they want someplace not overrun with similar stores."

"Yeah?" Jack scrunches his brow, apparently confused as to what Outdoorsmen Oasis has to do with the lodge.

"You've got, what, like a thousand acres?"

He leans back, his mouth slightly parted. "Actually, twelve hundred, give or take."

"Well?" I raise my hands and open my mouth in anticipation of his response.

"Bianca, are you suggesting that Outdoorsmen Oasis build here?" He taps his index finger on the countertop.

"Not where the lodge is." I laugh. Surely he didn't think I meant bulldoze this place? "You can sell some of your property that backs up to the four-lane to Macon and Ronald for the store."

Jack exhales, his nostrils flaring. "Bianca, I can't sell this land."

That wasn't the reaction I expected. "Not even fifty acres?"

"No." His jaw clenches and his eyes darken.

My skin tingles. "I understand your apprehension, but road frontage property this close to Tuscaloosa could bring in ten thousand an acre or better. That's you're payoff there. Plus, having a sporting goods store next to a hunting lodge . . ." I hold out my palms, metaphorically putting the ball in his court.

"It's not for sale."

"Could you let me run it by the guys first and see what they'd offer?"

"Doesn't matter." He stands and stares straight ahead. "You can't put a price on family land." He starts to leave.

"Jack, I—"

He stops at the doorway and turns. "Can we please not talk about this? I've got a lot to do before the morning."

My heart sinks as he walks away from a no-brainer deal —and from me. I glance down at my bowl of melting ice cream. Thanks to my parents and now this train wreck of a suggestion to Jack, I can't stomach even one bite. I sit in silence, observing a line of ice cream as it trickles down the honeybun.

Footsteps echo from beside me. My heart lifts. Jack must've had a change of heart about the land or at least about the way he left things with me.

I lift my head to Ronald, which tanks my heart again.

"Hey there. Got any more of those honeybuns left?"

I shift my eyes toward the pan Jack brought in, which lies

empty aside from some caramelized sugar. "Here you go." I slide my bowl toward him.

Maybe he'll accept the melted mess or maybe not. I don't stick around to find out. I step outside and resume my spot at the edge of the patio. Unlike earlier, I welcome the cold stone beneath my legs. Cold air always numbs my skin. And that's the perfect way to take the focus off the numbness I feel inside.

I can't control my parents or Jack. But I can control my part in all this drama. I stand and let out a heavy sigh. No matter what, I refuse to fight with Jack. I care about him too much to leave Alabama without letting him know what he means to me.

And, regardless of what he thinks, I won't give up on helping him turn the lodge into a success.

CHAPTER TWELVE

Jack

I cup my hands around my mouth and breathe warm air into them as I walk up the front porch. I open the front door, then Ronald and Macon walk past me, shedding their caps and overcoats.

"You guys ready for some breakfast?"

"Always." Ronald grins and pats his stomach.

"Okay, I'm gonna build a fire, then I'll make some eggs and bacon."

"Thanks, Jack." Macon nods.

"You bet." I close the door and busy myself building a fire as the men settle back in the leather recliners. Once the flames catch, I close the grate and head for the kitchen.

Everything is quiet this time of day. Except for Ronald bossing Macon about what they should watch on TV. I enjoy early hunts and mornings in general. The quietness gives me a rare opportunity to reflect without feeling rushed.

I remove my coat and wash my hands, admiring the way the sun shines through the glass doors. Paying this place off will be an uphill battle, but I'll find a way to manage. Any way other than selling off part of the property.

When my grandfather died, the family discussed what to do with all the property. Dad and Uncle Jeremy wanted to sell the small cabin and surrounding acreage, keeping most of it for themselves to hunt and camp. Then, I offered to buy the cabin and manage the land. John and Jeremy Jackson have their hands full with the family hardware store, and both prefer to spend their spare time hunting or watching sports. Not mending fences or making sure Apple Cart's teenagers don't sneak onto the place for unsolicited prom parties and such.

Me moving in and fixing up everything Grandpa had let fall to the wayside seemed like a great solution.

And it had been. That is until I got stars in my eyes and decided to build a mansion within spitting distance of the shop. Talk about biting off more than I can chew.

I crack some eggs in a bowl. Maybe I should get a chicken coop, as many eggs as we go through in a week. But then I'd have chickens to take care of, too. I gaze out the window. The view helps calm my nerves. It's too early to worry. I'll focus on the beauty of God's creations instead.

Speaking of beauty, Bianca strolls into the kitchen and sits at the island.

"Well, good morning. You're up early."

She shrugs. "I didn't want to waste my last day here." Her green eyes lock with mine as a smile spreads across her face. Good. I had worried for a second she might hold last night against me. Surely she understands my desire to hold onto something sentimental.

I turn my attention back to the bacon before it burns. "You hungry?"

"A little."

"I can make you some eggs that aren't cooked in bacon grease if you like."

She laughs. "I appreciate that, but I need to make another smoothie to finish up what kale and broccoli I have left."

"Yeah, I don't know if deer eat kale." I glance at her as I put the bacon on a paper towel.

"You could eat it."

I wrinkle my nose and shake my head. "Turnip greens are close enough for me."

She laughs again, sending a tiny ping against my chest. How I'll miss her laugh. Her smile. Her rosy scent. Her.

"Jack, I'm sorry about last night."

Ugh, then don't bring it up. "It's fine, really."

"No, I should've been more understanding. And I want you to know I'm available to help with more plans if you want to talk about it."

"Thanks, but I'm good for now." I smile at her and hope to God she'll drop it.

She circles the island and stands in front of me. "Where are the guys?"

"Probably still watching TV. If you'd come down a little earlier, you'd have heard Ronald tossing out orders as to why the deathly fishing series was superior to those trucker shows."

A mischievous grin crosses her face. She peers around the refrigerator toward the kitchen opening. Then, she pulls me back a little so that both of us are against the counter, our faces hidden from the hallway.

Her eyes dance with something a little wild that drives me crazy. Before I can say anything, she bats her eyelashes and presses her lips to mine. My lips tighten. What if someone walks in? But as soon as she folds her arms around my neck, I'm gone.

I drop my spatula and cup her face, tilting her head to kiss her deeper. The fish mitt holds my other hand captive, so I rest it on the small of her back.

She continues kissing me as if she might never have the chance to again. And I kiss her harder, knowing that this in fact might be my last chance to kiss her. Who cares if Ronald, or even Macon, walks in? We're all adults, and a simple kiss shouldn't ruin anyone's business at this point.

But this is no simple kiss. This is *the* kiss. The one that makes my emotions spill over.

We continue kissing until I smell something burning behind us. I pulled back, and Bianca screeches.

I had been leaning against the stove burner, and my shirt is on fire. I beat at the flame with my oven mitt. But instead of extinguishing my shirt, my precious fish mitt bursts into flames. In a panic, I rip off my T-shirt and throw it in the sink, along with the mitt. Thank God for old, dry-rotted material.

I fling the faucet knobs on and watch as the flames turn to singe and smoke beneath the stream of water. I sink back against the counter opposite of the stove and sigh, running a hand through my hair.

Once my heart rate and the hairs on my arms have lowered, I look at Bianca. She smiles as if she hasn't just set me on fire. In more ways than one. "Why are you smiling?"

Her eyes scan my body before meeting my face. "Your abs are tighter than I imagined." She waves her hand toward the stove. "What with all the grease and honeybuns you eat."

I shrug. "Well, I work." Then, I glance back at the stove, remembering the eggs. "Shoot."

I picked up the spatula from where it fell on the counter and rake at the eggs. They don't budge. I puff out my cheeks and set the pan in the sink on top of the smoky shirt rags. Then, I turn off the faucet. If any fire remains by now, I'll count my losses and collect insurance on the place.

"It looks like we'll all be eating eggs without grease today." I slide past Bianca and open the refrigerator door.

"That's where I smell smoke." Ronald's voice rings out from the hallway. "I knew it wasn't the fireplace. What—"

He walks up and stares at me like I've lost my mind instead of my shirt. "Happened in here?"

"Short answer, I've got to make more eggs." I grab a carton of eggs and shut the refrigerator door. "Long answer, I burnt the eggs, set myself on fire, tossed my flaming shirt in the sink, and ruined my favorite oven mitt." I frown.

He remains silent while I start a fresh pan of eggs. This time, I give them my full attention. And after I scramble them to perfection, using butter instead of bacon grease, I set out some plates and forks.

"I have bacon and eggs. You can help yourselves. I'm going to run home and change." I drop my gaze to my bare chest. "Or just put on more clothes."

I grab my coat and shrug it on, even though I'm not the least bit cold. Thanks to the recent fire and Bianca's steamy kiss.

"Be back in a bit." I reach in the sink for my burnt apparel and exit out the back door.

I toss my soiled shirt and mitt in the bed of my truck and climb in the driver's seat. I crank the truck and laugh at my shirtless open-jacket look. If I shave my chest and gain twenty pounds of muscle, I can look like the cover of a romance novel. But no need to do that, as Bianca has already complimented my abs.

My pulse races at the memory of our last kiss. Last kiss. Those words pound in my head and heart. I don't want this to end, and I'd planned on telling her that after our kiss. Then, I'd gone and caught myself on fire like an idiot.

Sometime before she leaves, I'll get her alone and express my feelings. Not just with a kiss but also with words. Ask her if we could try long distance. For her, I'll willingly visit Atlanta whenever I can.

The practical side of me comes up with a million reasons why we shouldn't be together. We come from not only two different locations but two different worlds. I felt an attraction to her from day one. But that was all superficial. Now I am close to falling for her.

I haven't connected with a woman on this level in years. And if Bianca can learn to shoot a gun and forego makeup, then I can do what is needed to keep her.

Bianca

I swallow the rest of my smoothie and scan the papers spread across my desk. We have one last meeting, so I want to tie up as many loose ends as possible while we're all here. Locations in Florida, Georgia and Mississippi are well underway, which only leaves Alabama open.

If only Jack wasn't so stubborn. I could make my clients happy and give him financial freedom in one fell swoop. I bend over the Alabama papers for a closer look. I'd begrudgingly listed two alternative locations after Jack's dismissal of my perfect plan. But neither is as centrally located as Apple Cart.

The guy's sitting on a gold mine but is too headstrong to mine it.

I massage my temples. I have no other choice. I'll present both alternatives to Macon and Ronald. Maybe one will fly.

I straighten and stack the papers, filing them into a folder. For the first time in days, I curl my hair and apply all my makeup. Sooner than I want, I'll be on my way to Atlanta. My camouflage casual won't be as welcome there.

I gather my folders and laptop, along with my empty smoothie glass. My heels click across the wooden surface as I make my way downstairs. I set my glass by the kitchen sink and cross the hall to the conference room. Macon is already seated at the head of the table.

Ronald comes bolting in behind me, a bag of Cheetos in his hand. "I'm coming. Needed a snack."

"Breakfast was an hour ago." Macon lifts a hand and wrinkles his forehead.

"Well, I'm a growing boy." Ronald opens the bag and pops a cheese curl in his mouth. "I just won't say which way I'm growing."

I laugh as Macon rolls his eyes. I'll miss these guys almost as much as I'll miss Jack. Except that I'll still be in constant contact with them. A hollowness pits my stomach. Will I ever see Jack after this?

"Where are we on locations, Bianca?"

My eyes widen as I open the folder. I need to stop pining over Jack and focus on business. At least for now.

"Yes, I have pinpointed the best locations for optimal traffic in all these states." I lick my index finger and shuffle through the papers, handing a copy of each to both Ronald and Macon. "There's a sheet for each location with details on the population and land prices. I tried to find a place centrally located in each state that also welcomes new industries, which should get you a better deal."

"This is great." Macon turns the pages, scanning each one. "I see you've got two locations for Alabama. That will be great later on, but we don't want to get ahead of ourselves with too many stores in one state."

"Oh, yeah. Those are your two options. One is in the northern part of the state and the other's closer to the coast. They both have their benefits."

"What about here?"

I take a deep breath.

"Have you talked to Jack?" Ronald speaks around a mouth full of Cheetos.

I let out the breath and lift my shoulders, preparing to explain why Jack doesn't want to sell without saying too much. "I have."

"And?" Ronald chews louder the more silence passes between us.

"He doesn't want to sell."

"I'm sure you made it clear we only want a small portion near the interstate, right?" Macon frowns at the papers in front of him, clearly set on Jack's land.

Disappointment looms in the air with both Macon trying to hide a frown and Ronald acting uncharacteristically quiet. My pulse picks up. I pride myself in always finding the best for my clients. And if I didn't care for Jack on such a personal level, I would continue pushing him to sell until he gave in to get me off his back.

I can't let my personal life get in the way of business. Dad would see it as me putting my own preferences above the client's once again. "I can talk to him again. I'm sure if I approach it differently, I can persuade him to see things our way."

Macon smiles, and Ronald stops chewing. I force a half-smile, but my nerves twist inside. So much for pleasing both parties at the same time. That ship has long set sail.

The entire mood of the meeting shifts once I agree to persuade Jack to sell. Only problem, I don't want to persuade him to sell. Not that I've had a change of heart about it being a great idea. More like I don't want to spend my last few hours with Jack talking shop and crushing his spirits.

Too bad my job—current and future—depends on me doing so.

I grab a bottle of water out of the refrigerator and head outside. The weather is mild, so I welcome sitting outside to make a call this time. My phone vibrated once during the meeting with a missed call from Dad. I've got a little time left before lunch to fill him in on everything.

I pull a chair over to the edge of the patio, not wanting to sit on the ground in my slacks. I've foregone the jeans and boots today as if metaphorically transitioning myself back to Atlanta. "Hello, Dad."

He answers with a happier-than-usual tone. That's always a good sign.

"The guys signed some contracts for us to manage their accounts and help with overseeing their expansion."

I smile as he praises my efforts. He asks a few questions about the lodge and my time here. I tell him about hunting and the rustic mansion, which leads to more questions.

"How about I video call you and show you the place?"

He agrees, and I hang up and redial as a video chat. When he answers, I wave the phone slowly behind me so that he can see the place. "I would show you the front, but we would lose service on the way. There's only two spots where I can get a signal."

"That's fine. It's lovely." He smiles approvingly. "I'm very proud of you for taking on this client. You've shown real growth in getting out of your comfort zone."

My cheeks warm. Dad doesn't dish out compliments easily. So when he says something positive, you know he means it. "Thanks, Dad. You have no idea how much it means for me to hear you say that."

"I'm serious." He clears his throat. "I would've given you more responsibility sooner, but I wanted you to prove yourself first."

I chew on the end of my fingernail. Is this his way of saying I've earned my spot as heir to the business?

"You're an intelligent girl, but some of your choices have been rather selfish and not best for everyone."

I narrow my eyes, a little put off by that statement. Where is he going with this?

"I'm not the best at sharing feelings, as you know." I nod. Me and everyone else who's ever met him. "But you've come a long way from the girl who turned down any client she wouldn't buy from. And a really long way from the girl who eloped with that prep-school pretty-boy."

I sigh, surprised to find myself smiling. My dad has a weird way of bringing up someone's sins while he praises their sainthood.

"You've proven with this trip that you're a selfless young woman, and I'm proud of you."

"Thank you." I rest my chin in my hand and hold the phone out once more for him to take in the view. "Maybe we can have more meetings here. It's a great quiet place to work."

"I'll make note of that. Be careful traveling back."

"Okay, bye." I wave to my phone screen before ending the call.

I stand and stare at the land in front of me. You can't find a view like this in Atlanta. And despite all the sushi bars and boutiques I adore, I've come to appreciate the slower pace, gazing at the stars from my balcony rather than street lights from my apartment window.

After taking a long moment to soak in my surroundings,

I turn to go inside. As I pull the chair back toward the center of the patio, I spot Jack by the back door cooking on the grill. My mouth goes dry. How long has he been there?

With my dad on speakerphone and sitting so far from the door, I didn't hear him come outside. But did he hear my conversation with Dad?

My throat closes as I recall my dad's words: "the girl who eloped with that prep-school pretty-boy." Of all people, Jack couldn't know about my elopement. Nothing good could come of that. Besides, we'd had our union annulled two days later. It wasn't like I got an actual divorce. Right?

I twist a lock of my hair and tiptoe toward the door. With any luck, he didn't hear Dad. Or at least not clear enough to make out what he said.

By the time I make it across the large patio, Jack has stepped inside with a platter of food. I rock back, my muscles loosening a bit. I want a few minutes to pass before I face Jack again. Just in case he heard something that could alter his opinion of me.

Even more than I wasn't ready to approach him again about selling the land, I wasn't ready for him to discover my most immature mistake.

CHAPTER THIRTEEN

Jack

I keep my back to the door and busy myself slicing up steak for deer poppers. Had I known Bianca would be out back on the phone, I'd have grilled the steaks earlier. But had I grilled them earlier, I might not've walked by the conference room when I did. And had I not walked down the hall at that very moment, I never would've overheard her plan to talk me into selling my land.

I fumble with the collar of my shirt, my neck heating up with rage. She'd led me to believe she hadn't mentioned the land to Macon. Then, to hear them discussing it. To hear her bragging how she could persuade me.

Were all her kisses and lingering hugs a plot from the beginning to strike a deal?

I stab the knife hard against the cutting board as I take out my frustration on the deer meat. But there isn't enough deer on my property to blow off steam.

My property. Not Macon and Ronald's. Not Outdoorsmen Oasis property.

I push the chopped steak onto a plate and start in on the jalapeños. Maybe I should leave the seeds in to teach them all a lesson. Except the one person I want to get back at the most wouldn't even take the bait.

I should've known better than to trust a woman who eats like a rabbit. My mama raised me smarter than that.

But love does crazy things to a man. Love? I shudder at the word. Do I love Bianca? After our kiss this morning, I've considered using that word, strong as it sounds. It had stuck on the tip of my tongue, ready to fall out of my mouth the next time I saw her.

Too bad I overheard that conversation before seeing her alone. Or is it too bad? Maybe this is for my own good.

I lean back and peer through the window. No sign of Bianca. I expected her to have come in by now, but maybe she went around front. I relax a little.

A few more hours. Then she'll be gone. They'll all be gone. The three of them can conjure up deals for their stores elsewhere, and I can go on with my life. Lonely as it gets at times, this place has never hurt me. The land is my sanctuary, and I would die before giving it up.

I preheat the oven and stuff the peppers before meticulously wrapping them with bacon. I'd planned on mixing a salad with the lettuce and the last of Bianca's toppings. When I open the refrigerator, my anger gets the best of me.

I pull all her remaining healthy food from the refrigerator and chuck it in the trashcan. There. She can go hungry, for all I care. It won't kill her to wait for some vegan junk at the airport.

The oven beeps, and I reach for my fish mitt. My face drops. I regret the kiss that ended the life of my best kitchen companion, then reach for the flimsy oven mitt that the gas company gave me when they installed my stove.

Heat blows in my face when I open the oven door, causing sweat to bead up on my already flaming face. I toss both pans of poppers on the racks and slam the door. Tossing my cap on the counter, I run both hands up my face and rake them through my hair.

How stupid. I should've seen through someone like Bianca showing an interest in me. No wonder she'd been pleasantly surprised by my abs. I'm not her type!

I picture her dating guys wearing skinny jeans and sport coats, gelled hair and clean shaven. And not just their faces and chests, but their arms and possibly legs, too. What could she want with a hairy chested, lanky country boy? To further her business. That's what.

Yet, I'd allowed her to seduce me with those deep green eyes and long legs. The yoga pants hadn't helped my case either.

I only have myself to blame. Maybe I should've returned some of those casserole dishes in person or taken up Daisy Duncan's offer to spend a day out here and research scents for her woodsy candle collection. Any of the single Southern belles in town wouldn't have hurt my heart like Bianca. Even those who want nothing more than a God-fearing man to give them children one day.

The back door opens, making the hair on my arms stand up. I close my eyes, preparing to face the seductress head on.

"Hey, sugar. You look like you've been rode hard and put up wet."

Oh, thank God. I open my eyes, never so happy to hear Mrs. Mary's voice. I push myself away from the counter and take the box from her hand. "These look delicious."

"Thanks. I don't know what they prefer, so I brought a variety. Apple, lemon and pecan."

"No, that's perfect." I inhale the wonderful mixture of fruit and nuts. "As soon as the deer poppers go off, I'll get everyone in here to eat. You're welcome to join us."

"I appreciate it, but I can't stay too long. I need to do some bookwork before cooking for the dinner crowd."

"I understand." I set the box of pies on the counter.

"Jack?"

"Yes ma'am?"

"What's wrong?"

I look up and try to keep a neutral face. "What makes you say that?"

"When I walked in here, you looked a mess. Did you sleep any last night?"

"I slept fine."

"Then what's going on?"

I sigh and hoist myself onto the counter beside the pies. "Let's just say I let my guard down, and now I'm paying for it."

Mrs. Mary plants one hand on her hip and the other on the island. Her expression says she's ready to fight. "It's that girl, ain't it?"

I fidget with my collar, hesitating to answer. As much as I dislike Bianca right now, I don't want to unleash Mrs. Mary on her. But after a minute of her staring me down, I decide I'd rather redirect her wrath. I nod.

"I knew it." She slaps the island counter, making me flinch. "You're too good for some city slicker."

"Now, Mrs. Mary."

"What?" She props her other hand on her hip and scowls. "Jack Jackson, you need to recognize your worth. You are a smart, handsome young man, and a child of God. Some skinny skank like that don't deserve you."

I shake my head and laugh. She has quite a way with

words. "Mrs. Mary, please. It's not as bad as you think. I just let myself get a little too distracted by her . . ."

"Mmm hmm. I'm gonna pray for you, boy." She wags a finger toward me and smiles. "It's all gonna be all right. By this time tomorrow, that little vixen will be gone, and you'll never have to see her again."

"Yeah . . ." I sigh. Bianca leaving makes me both relieved and depressed at the same time. Come tomorrow, I could forget about her. Or could I? I welcome putting the business end of things behind me ASAP. Now, as for that kiss . . . and all the ones that came before it? Short of amnesia, I don't stand a chance of forgetting her.

The kiss replays in the back of my brain, raising my already heightened pulse. Then, the oven beeps, knocking me out of hypnosis.

I remove the deer poppers, then turn back to Mrs. Mary. "I'd better let everyone know it's time to eat. Thanks for the dessert."

She nods, dropping her hands from her hips in a slow surrender. "If you need me, sugar, for anything at all."

"Yes, ma'am. I appreciate it." And I do. But if I can't handle a willowy woman obsessed with making a deal, then I'm not sure I deserve to keep this place.

Bianca

The leaves on the trees start to swirl the longer I stare outside. Not wanting to run into Jack, I'd entered the house from the front and sneaked back upstairs. On my way up, I heard chopping noises in the kitchen.

Under normal circumstances, I would welcome the chance to talk with Jack while he cooks. Or maybe more than talk, even if it led to a small house fire. But I'm not ready to face him, not without knowing what he heard.

I toss my head back on the leathery chair near the window and tuck my legs beneath me. With no more meetings and a plane to catch later, I allow myself to rest. At least physically. My mind is a whirlwind of chaos.

When sitting proves more of a burden than a blessing to my mind, I get up and finish packing. I've packed everything except for all my soiled clothing and dirty boots. For those, I'll need something to shield my suitcase.

Jack may keep some trash bags in the hall linen closet. He has everything else in there, from scentless shampoo to toilet paper. I tiptoe down the hall, not caring to put on any shoes. I open the closet door and scan the shelves. Very organized. Not that I take Jack for a slob, but he does keep dog treats and empty Mountain Dew cans on the kitchen counter at his cabin.

I start at the top and work my way down, not finding the trash bags until I bend over and move a case of toilet paper aside. I roll off a bag, which turns out to be no larger than the one in my small bathroom trashcan. This will hold precisely one half of a boot. I tear off several more before standing up straight. When I do, my backside bumps into something. Jack?

I spin around and come nose to nose with Ronald. "Whoa, sorry, I . . ."

"Expecting someone else?" Ronald cocks an eyebrow.

I lift my shoulders. My cheeks heat up as I take a step back.

"Have you talked to your boy about the land again?"

"I . . . not yet. I haven't really had a chance."

He lifts his chin as if he doesn't believe me. I glance over his shoulder to see Jack walking up the stairs. "Maybe in a minute."

Ronald turns his head and nods at Jack.

Jack nods back. "Ronald, I was coming to tell you guys that lunch is ready downstairs."

"Thanks." Ronald passes Jack on the stairs, clearly not wanting to miss a meal.

Jack stops and stares at me. I have trouble reading his expression, but I can tell that it isn't a pleasant one. It's safe to say that the honeymoon phase has officially ended. Like it or not, I need to talk to him.

"Are you looking for something?"

I hold up a fistful of trash bags and shut the closet door. "Jack, can we talk?"

He shoves his hands in his pockets and shrugs before answering. "Okay."

I open the door to my room and motion for him to go in. Ronald has abandoned everything for food, and at this point it doesn't much matter if Macon sees the two of us alone in my room. Besides, he wants me to talk to Jack. Just not about what I have in mind.

I follow him inside and shut the door behind us. "Have a seat."

Jack pulls his hands out of his pockets and sits on the edge of the bed. I sit beside him, my skin crawling with an array of emotions. I want to kiss him, shake him, and slap him all at the same time.

"Jack, I don't know what you heard me say earlier today."

He huffs and crosses his arms. "I heard it all."

I rock back and forth slightly. I'd planned an answer for this in my head, but the sudden heaviness in my chest lodges the words inside. For a good guy like Jack, an annulment would mean a divorce all the same. I start with something vague to ease him in. "This all happened so long ago."

He balks. "Hardly. I heard it just hours ago."

My palms moisten. "Jack, I mean about when I got married."

He leaps to his feet. "You're married? And you cheated on your husband with *me*?"

"No." I grab his forearm. I can feel the rage inside him through his hot skin.

"Of all the lousy ways to swing a deal. You really will go to any lengths to make me sell this land, huh?" He drops his arms and starts to walk out.

I hop up and pull him back. He shrugs me off, but I get in his face. "No, listen. I'm very much single. But almost a decade ago, I was married for two days."

He lets out a tense laugh. "Two days?"

I nod and run a sweaty hand across my forehead. "I eloped the night of my high school graduation. When my parents discovered where I was and what I'd done, they made me get an annulment."

"Why are you telling me all this now? Because I bared my soul to you about my debt?" He jabs a finger at his chest with every word. "You think confessing some failed teenage relationship is gonna make me trust you again?"

I clutch my arms around my stomach. I think I'm going to be sick. "No, this has nothing to do with that. I thought you heard me saying—"

"What I heard was the three of you in the conference room chatting about how you were gonna persuade me to sell. I assume the plan was formed about the time you started kissing me."

"No." My vision blurs as tears fill my eyes. "Jack, there was no master plan. I thought of you selling after the kisses, while I was up late one night wracking my brain for ways to help you."

"Yeah, well I told you to drop it, and you spoke to them about it anyway."

"I mentioned it to Macon before I told you."

His nostrils flare as his eyes dart around the room, away from me. When his eyes meet mine again, they no longer have their sparkle. "Well, thanks for that."

"Jack, that's how business works. I present an idea to the client to see if they have any interest before I pursue further and get someone on the other end excited over nothing."

"Well, you got me real excited, Bianca." He shakes his head. "Excited about telling you how I feel, about visiting you in Atlanta, about seeing where this could go. But all I am to you is a piece of property. Real estate to make a buck."

"No, Jack." I lift my tingling hands. I reach for his shoulders, but he steps back, letting my hands fall. Tears run down my cheeks.

"Bianca, I can't." He removes his cap and messes with his hair. A gesture I find so endearing, but one that I've learned indicates his frustration.

"Jack, please. I think I love you." My heart aches as the words crawl from my creaky throat.

"Oh, you think so? We've already established that you'll say anything for business."

He opens the door and stares at me. His soft blue eyes are now cold crystals that stab my heart like an icepick. "I'll arrange a ride to the airport for you."

I swallow back new tears as I watch him leave. I can't allow myself to cry anymore. The damage is done, and I need to appear strong to Macon and Ronald. The downside of being a woman in business is needing to overcompensate for being a woman in business.

As soon as I can convince my legs to work, I cross the room and finish packing. Shoving boots into plastic bags helps relieve a smidge of my tension. And knowing that all the mud on my clothing is indirectly due to Jack makes shoving them in trash bags all the more appealing.

By the time I've packed everything, my mood has transitioned from sad to mad. My tears have dried, and, thanks to waterproof mascara, my face remains unscathed.

I grab my turquoise luggage, laptop bag, and purse. Trudging down the massive staircase is quite the obstacle. But I'll die before asking Jack for help.

My bag hits the floor with a thud. I'm so relieved to reach ground level that I don't mind that my expensive travel bag might be maimed. I wipe my sweaty palms on my pants and blow a loose hair out of my eye.

Laughter drifts down the hallway from the kitchen. I hold my stomach. I need to say goodbye to Macon and Ronald. But can I hold it together with Jack close by?

I raise my head high and scold myself for all but falling apart over Jack. I've talked down men twice my age over million-dollar deals. Yet, I've allowed a carefree country boy get the best of me.

Lifting my shoulders, I drag my bags toward the door, then proceed to the kitchen. Everyone sits around the island, eating a variety of pies. I adjust my purse strap and lean against the back counter.

"Would you like some pie?" The nonchalance in Jack's voice pricks a tiny hole in my heart.

"No, thank you." How can he sit there and eat like we didn't just fight upstairs? And how can he expect me to do the same? "Your ride should be here soon."

I nod and force a pleasant face for Macon and Ronald's sake. My eyes drift toward the window. Last night, I dreaded leaving this place. But since then . . .

Choking back a tear, I open the refrigerator and take out

a bottle of water. I don't want a drink as much as I want to hide my face. And the coolness helps to dry my tear ducts.

I shut the door and swallow a huge gulp of water. Ronald and Macon sit in silence, stuffing their faces. My nerves twitch at the quietness.

"Macon, before I go, do you guys have all my numbers?" I'd given them my business card and contact info on day one. But saying something stupid helps to drown out the awkwardness in the air.

"Yes, ma'am. Thanks again for getting the ball rolling on all this."

"Sure thing." I smile, this time not so forced. I glance around another minute and adjust my purse strap again to have something to do.

Then, the doorbell rings, sending a melody through the front of the house. Jack goes to answer it and returns with his friend. Tanner, maybe?

"Miss Manderson, I'll be escorting you to the airport." He bows and gives me a dimpled grin.

Just peachy. Jack must really want rid of me to recruit this tool for help.

"Tanner has a little time, since his schedule is flexible, so he can drive you."

"And my man owes me a poker debt as well." Tanner slaps Jack's shoulder.

So now I'm a payoff for a personal debt. Perfect. I glare at Jack, searching for an answer. Did he really change his opinion of me so much, so soon? Or did he never care for me at all?

The hollowness in his eyes reveals nothing. An emotionless void. I turn toward Macon and Ronald and extend my hand. One by one, they shake it. "It was a pleasure. We'll be in touch."

"Yes, ma'am. Take care." Macon smiles, and Ronald smiles best he can with a mouthful of pie.

As I walk toward the kitchen exit, I turn around, giving Jack one last chance to show anything at all. Love, hate, disgust, happiness, relief. Anything but nothing.

Instead, he clenches his jaw and lifts his chin. And that in itself tells me everything.

CHAPTER FOURTEEN

Jack

"Jack, are you gonna fold?"

I glance up at Jonah then down at my cards. My head hasn't been in the game all night, and this round, I haven't even cared to look at my cards. "Uh, no. I'm in."

I don't have the best hand, but I may as well play. Anything to try to distract myself from Bianca.

Jonah and Tanner toss their cards on the table. I do the same, laying down the worst hand ever. Yeah, I should've folded. Tanner rakes the chips with his arm and lets out a mock evil laugh.

"Jack, where you at, man?" Jonah grabs a handful of chips and stares me down as he chews.

"No, leave him alone. I like how he's playing." Tanner's evil laugh returns.

"I'm sure you do." I roll my eyes and rest my hands behind my head.

"Seriously though, what's with you tonight?" Jonah waves a hand in front of my face, coming dangerously close to dusting my nose with Doritos dust.

"I don't know."

"I do." Tanner chugs the rest of his sweet tea and slams the plastic cup on the table.

"Well, somebody tell me." Jonah lifts his palms and glances at me, then Tanner.

"He's not been the same since Bianca left."

I grunt, steam coming from my nostrils. "You don't know what happened."

"I know enough to know that's what caused whatever this is." Tanner leans across the table and stares at me.

"Huh?" Jonah looks to me for an answer.

I pick up my own cup and walk to the refrigerator. "It's nothing personal. Just business."

"Yeah, well. I think Blondie took it personal. She didn't say two words all the way to the airport. Any other woman who spends over an hour of quality time with me would've been eating out of my hand by now." Tanner palms a handful of chips and tosses them in his mouth.

I want to puke. "Or could it be that some women don't like men who come on to them every waking minute with pickup lines cheesier than your breath." I point the sweet tea jug toward Tanner before refilling my cup.

"Looky there, Jonah, I struck a chord in our boy." Tanner grins.

I sit back down and fold my arms across my chest. "You did not strike a chord. I'm just trying to drive home the point that there is nothing between Bianca and me other than business."

"Okay, whatever man." Tanner shakes his head.

"What kind of business?" Jonah talks around a mouthful of chips.

I run my hands down my face. "You too? What is this, an intervention?"

"No, I'm just worried about you. That's all. I knew something was different soon as I walked in this afternoon."

"Okay, ladies. Hold onto your panties while I spill the tea." I lean my elbows on the table and narrow my eyes at Tanner. "And I need no side comments." He points to himself and balks.

"I was doing some cleaning and stuff on their last day at the lodge. I was at the closet by the conference room getting a broom when I overheard them talking about me."

"Them who?" Jonah perks up like a child at story time.

"The Outdoorsmen Oasis guys and Bianca. They were having a meeting about their stores."

"Then why would they talk about you?" Tanner just couldn't stay quiet.

I hold up a finger to shush him. "Bianca tried to get me to sell some of the back acreage to them for a new store."

"And?"

"And?" I huff. "I told her no. And as if that wasn't enough, she let on like she hadn't mentioned it to them but clearly by their conversation, she had." Tanner's mouth parts, and I hold up my finger again. "I swear Tanner, the next finger I hold up won't be a nice one."

His lips smack shut, and I drop my hand. "As I was saying, Bianca went as far as to say she could convince me to see things their way."

"That's not nice." Jonah snarls.

"No, it isn't." I take a sip of tea and wipe the back of my hand across my mouth. "And now all I can think about is that everything she said was premeditated. Every kiss a trap."

"Whoa." Tanner jumps up, knocking his chair to the floor. "She kissed you?"

My ears grow hot. I hadn't meant for that to leak out,

especially with Tanner in the room. Tanner claps his hands and laughs.

Jonah leans over to me and whispers, "Now's the time to show that other finger."

I shake my head. "That was my fault. Slip of the tongue."

"I'll say." Tanner circles the table and punches my arm with his fist. "You sly dog."

"Stop." Jonah gets between us.

"What?" Tanner steps back and opens his arms.

"Can't you see he's a mess?"

"Thanks, cuz." I narrow my eyes at Jonah.

"Well, bud, you are. And I see why. You don't know if this girl was using you or really liked you."

I nod. "And she wanted me to sell our grandpa's land."

"Well, how much of it?"

This time I get in Jonah's face. "Does it matter how much? An inch or a mile, it's our land."

Jonah plops down in his seat and stares at the ceiling. "Oh, here we go."

"What?" I scowl.

"Come on, Jack. Our dads would've sold the place already if you hadn't moved out here. You know that. You're the only one who sees this land as sacred."

"And why is that, Jonah?" I motion toward the back door that leads out to the hunting land. "Our grandparents worked their tails off for this place."

"To provide for all of us." Jonah steadies his jaw the way he does when he feels he has the upper hand.

This was no poker face, though. And I knew he was right.

Tanner raises his hand and waves at me. "May I speak without getting a finger in my face."

"Why not?" I motion for Tanner to take the floor and sit back in my seat.

"You said Bianca wanted you to sell some of the land, right?"

"Yeah." The frustration comes through loud and clear in my tone.

"Then if you sell some and keep the rest, isn't that like having your ice cream and eating it, too?"

"Cake," Jonah calls from across the table.

"Huh?" Tanner makes the same face he made in high school Algebra.

"It's cake. Have your cake and eat it, too. The adage is cake."

"Whatever, ice cream still makes my point." Tanner pulls up a chair and sits in front of me. "How much land we talkin' here?"

"Around fifty acres."

Tanner steeples his fingers and stares at the ceiling a minute. "Now I'm no mathematician, but don't y'all have like a million acres?"

"A thousand." Jonah answers.

"Actually, it's closer to twelve-hundred." I can't help but correct him. To me, every hundred acres counts. Every fifty acres counts.

"See, more reason to not worry over fifty." Jonah nods at me.

I bury my head in my hands and moan. I take a long breath and exhale before raising my head. "I had big plans for that land. I wanted to build a pond and a shooting range."

"And you still can." Tanner shrugs. "If I owned all this, we'd already have put in a drive-in theatre. Those things make bank."

"I don't want to commercial up the place." I peer out the window. Even in the dark, I enjoy the view. Pitch darkness means no street lights or neon signs.

"Yeah, well, the way I see it, you've already commercialized it." Jonah snatches the bag of chips from the table and gives me another know-it-all stare.

"Why would you say that?"

"Come on, Jack. People pay you to stay here. You built a log cabin Taj Mahal and have Mrs. Mary carting cornbread through here like it's a bed and breakfast."

My nostrils flare. As mad as Jonah's words make me, they hit home. Literally, my home. Which I pimp out to hunters.

I lower my eyes, not wanting to face my cousin. "You're right."

"I am?"

"Yeah." I lift my face. Jonah's eyes widen in surprise.

"Boy, I've waited half my life to hear you say that." He beams with pride.

"You're not the only one." Tanner cuts his eyes toward me and smirks.

"Thanks, *best* friends."

"Hey, we are because we're honest." Tanner raises his cup at Jonah.

"Whatever." I shake my head. "I guess in hindsight fifty acres, isn't so bad. It could put me in a better place financially."

"So you're not mad at Blondie?"

"I don't know." I say that more to myself than Tanner. The land stuff, I can shrug off. The kisses, I can't.

Bianca

I wiggle my toes, relaxing as the jets massage them. Too bad the salon doesn't offer deep scrubs on brain cells. Nice as it is, a spa pedicure can only go so far to soothe my head.

"What's been up with you?"

"You're our HR lady and my best friend, so you tell me." There. Way to redirect Ariel's prying. If this money management business ever folds, I might consider politics.

"Bianca." Ariel twists in her massage chair, then quickly straightens when the girl filing her nails jerks her hand back into place. "Sorry." Ariel smiles at the manicurist, then shifts her head toward me, this time keeping the rest of her body still. "You haven't been the same since you came back from camp nowhere."

"It always takes me a few days to readjust from traveling. You know that." I lift my legs from the water and exhale slowly while the man working on my feet rubs grainy lotion up to my calves.

"Bianca, it's been a few days. And we both know that's not always true. Last trip, you came back in a better mood than you were in when you left."

I frown at her. "That's because I'd spent a week in New York surrounded by makeup."

"Okay, I see your point. But something happened down there in Alabama." Ariel points a finger my way. "And you're not telling me." She scrunches her perfectly shaped brows at me, then moans at the smudge she's created on her not-so-dry nails. She shrugs at her manicurist and lays her hand back on the arm rest. The girl sighs and starts smoothing out the pink glob on Ariel's cuticle.

I should've come alone. Any stress relief brought on by the warm towels wrapped around my legs vanishes with Ariel's accusations. I close my eyes, pondering what will happen if I toss the towels aside and run out of the spa, gritty bare feet pounding the marble floors. I raise one leg in protest, then think better of myself when the guy grabs my other foot and starts sloughing off dead skin. Yep, I'm stuck here, and Ariel knows it.

"I wasn't able to tie off one of the loose ends on store expansions."

"Well, nobody expects you to tie everything up with a nice little bow in one week of meetings. Who do you think you are, the Proverbs 31 woman?"

"Huh?" I hate it when she talks in code.

"You need to read your Bible."

I roll my eyes. "You sound like my mother."

"How's Janet doing, by the way? She hasn't stopped by the office in a while."

I rub the newly formed chill bumps on my arms. I'm not ready to discuss my parents' drama with anyone. Not with Ariel, and especially not with my parents. "She's good." I hug myself to pass the chill bumps off as coldness rather than panic.

"Good to know." Ariel smiles at me, then down at her nails.

Yeah, it would be good to know. I can't decide if I just lied to Ariel since my mom downplays everything. And I don't have the guts to ask Mom point-blank what's going on.

"Now, we need to get you good." Ariel wiggles her newly painted fingers and admires her ring.

She hasn't been married long at all, and counting the engagement, her ring is maybe two years old. I wonder how long I'd stare at it that way. Even more, I wonder if I'll ever even have a chance to stare at a ring that way. An impulsive elopement didn't exactly qualify for a diamond ring. Rich had slid his class ring on my finger and secured the extra room with my hair ribbon. Ah, young love. So immature and pathetic.

One thing I know for sure, when and *if* I ever marry again, it will be forever.

"According to my feet, I'm feeling pretty good." I relax my shoulders and sink back into the massage chair.

"Yeah, but this is temporary, my friend. You need something or *someone* in your life to keep you good."

"I have you." I smile at Ariel and bat my eyelashes.

"Ha, ha." She stares at the ceiling, shaking her head. "As flattering as that is, I think you need a man in your life."

"I—"

"Shhh. No sarcasm." She scolds.

I press my lips together. I may as well let her have her say so that we can all get on with our lives.

"Toby met this really nice guy at a fundraiser. Ryan something. They started playing golf together. He's around our age, never been married, tall."

I sigh as I try to ignore the "never been married" comment. Of course, Ariel doesn't mean anything by that, but it's still a touchy subject for me. I counter it in my head with the fact that he's tall. Any girl with long legs and a closet full of stilettos can appreciate that. "What are you suggesting?"

Ariel's full lips curve the moment the words leave my mouth. My friend smiles so big that her eyebrows disappear behind her dark bangs.

"A date." Ariel twists, careful to hold her hands still this time. "Ooh, a double-date if you want."

I bite my bottom lip and mull this over. Ariel will bug me to no end until I agree to at least have dinner with the man. But a double-date would mean having Ariel there, constantly checking my mood. Along with multiple visits to the ladies' room to ask what I thought of him. "I'm fine with a one-on-one date."

"Ooh. Look at you, now." Ariel flips her black hair over

one shoulder, then cringes as a few strands stick to her nails. She picks them off, one by one, and grits her teeth at the girl who is now polishing her toes. The manicurist ignores her this time, which is probably for the best.

I laugh at Ariel's excitement. "Calm down. I was only implying that I don't need a chaperone."

Her face resembles that of a cartoon villain as her eyes sparkle with something mischievous. I look down at my teal green toenails and wonder what I just signed up for.

I swallow hard and glare across the room at the wall full of nail polish. So many choices. Almost as many as the single men floating around Atlanta. Too bad I have no interest in dating anyone who isn't Jack. And the glacier blue of his eyes isn't exactly an option.

For my nails or my heart.

CHAPTER FIFTEEN

Jack

I pull a load of towels from the washer and shove them in the dryer. Thanks to sleeping in, I've had little time before church to do anything other than feed both my dogs and Freckles.

"Freckles." I shake my head as if that will dislodge the name from my brain. Freckles is just one more word to remind me of the one word I really want to forget—Bianca. What kind of name is that anyway?

A city girl name, that's what.

I toss in a dryer sheet, which Mom taught me will battle static. Then, unlike she taught me, I slam the dryer so hard, it jumps.

I sigh, happy to take my frustration out on something besides the dirt pile target. I press the dryer button and run a hand through my hair. Everything has been nonstop since I came home from church, and I still have a ton more to do before my new guests arrive.

For the next few days, I'm hosting a group of friends celebrating a retirement. They're from just across the Mississippi state line, and the guy who booked the reservation sounds entertaining. Not unlike Ronald.

Ronald. One more word that leads back to Bianca. I clear my throat and finish restocking all the bathrooms with toilet paper and soap. Staying busy might keep her off my mind. Even if the scentless shampoo makes me long for her rosy smell. I set the shampoo bottle on the tub shelf and jerk the curtain closed.

I plop down on the toilet seat and stare at the ceiling. Why did I ever let my guard down with that woman? Unfortunately, I don't have time to sit on the can and lament my sorrows. The clock is ticking, and I still need to sweep the front porch and cook deer poppers.

I rush downstairs, glancing at the living room clock on my way down. As I round the hallway, metal clanking echoes from the kitchen. What on earth?

I sneak around the corner, prepared to draw one of the dozen guns I have hidden around the house if need be. But that isn't necessary as I find Jonah rummaging through the bottom cabinets.

"What are you doing here?"

He glances over his shoulder, then stands. "I was headed back to Auburn and thought you might need some help before the next guests arrive."

I frown. Ever since my involuntary heart-to-heart with Jonah and Tanner Friday night, the guys have acted as if I'm a broken bottle and they're the duct tape needed to fix me.

"Come on, Jack. I know you've been working all weekend for this big group. I just want to help my cuz."

"You helped me load corn yesterday."

Jonah huffs and stretches out his hands. "For like two hours. Then I hunted with Dad the rest of the day."

I nod. That is true, and I could use the help. "All right, Cinderella, could you be a darlin' and sweep the front porch?"

"I was gonna make some loaded potato skins first. The girls love them at all the tailgates. And potatoes would go great with deer poppers."

I sigh. "Fine, but don't hog the oven. I have to cook four pans of deer poppers by six o'clock."

"Whatever you say, master." Jonah mocks a curtsey and laughs. I roll my eyes and go to grab a broom. I'll sweep the porch myself.

I step outside and breathe in the cool air. Cold weather makes for the best deer hunting. Maybe I'll find an excuse to get out early before everyone else tomorrow morning and watch the sunrise. I've done that a lot lately, which was partly to blame for me sleeping in this morning.

Something about sitting alone in nature with nothing but my thoughts and prayers gives me peace. Or, as was the case this weekend, my thoughts have brought on prayers for peace. As well as for guidance.

Jonah and Tanner have displayed their fair share of dislike for Bianca over the past two days, but they haven't talked about the land. Maybe because they know it is more than just land to me. Or maybe they can sense my confusion about why I view it that way.

No matter how I spin it, I have made the place somewhat of a tourist attraction. If only Grandpa were here. I'd ask his opinion on the whole store dilemma and find out once and for all if he cared for me selling the back acreage.

Macon and Ronald's stay last week covered this month's mortgage. I paid it a few weeks late, but still, I made it. But how much longer can I keep this place running paycheck to paycheck? Even a large group like today won't put me ahead. Not with the cost of utilities and food for that many people in a place this large.

I brush the last bit of dust off the porch and raise a fist to my mouth. Biting my knuckles, I look out at the land. I envy the days of carefree camping and hunting. Now everything leads back to costs and payments and keeping this place running. Adulting is no fun. And, in a way, it's sucked the fun out of this place.

In my mind, if I could keep all the land, I could somehow keep that childlike innocence of it all. No work, all play. But that's all a big illusion. And whenever I think otherwise, my pocketbook proves me wrong.

Bianca

I fluff my hair and check my makeup once more. Then, I laugh at myself for doing so. What does it matter? This date is half to get Ariel off my back and half to forget about Jack.

Ugh. Jack. That's why.

If a handsome man treats me to a nice meal and compliments my appearance, maybe, just maybe, I can push aside the scraggly guy who cooks everything in bacon grease. Yep, that's the plan.

I puff up my cheeks and hold my stomach. The sheer thought of Jack nauseates me. How could I have messed things up so badly? What I wouldn't give to reverse any mention of him selling his property. Then, maybe I'd be having dinner with him before he drove back to Alabama after a weekend visit.

I exhale and drop my hand. What's done is done, and I have no other option but to move on with tonight's plan. I turn off the bathroom lights and walk to the front of my apartment. I grab my purse from the kitchen counter and lock up on my way out.

An older couple shuffles down the hall in front of me. My face lifts when the man wraps a withered hand around the woman's shoulder. They stop at the elevator and gaze at one another sweetly as he hits the down button.

I wonder how long they've been together. Ten years, twenty years, thirty? Or are they rare unicorns still on their first marriage, until death do them part? Whatever the case, I can sense their love and admiration for one another.

The elevator door opens, and the couple steps inside. I get in behind them and hit the bottom floor button. They nod at me, and I return the gesture. Then, I drop my eyes to my fresh pedicure and gold-heeled sandals. Why couldn't finding the right man be as easy as picking the right nail polish?

The shimmer on my toenails glistens as the sun shines through the glass elevator door. After settling on the bottom floor, the elevator dings. I lift my eyes just enough to watch the couple's feet shuffle forward. Then, I raised my head and trot toward the apartment exit.

One thing I've learned over the years is to always drive myself on a first date. That leaves no expectations for how long I have to stay. If at any time I need to bail on the guy, my sapphire Mercedes coupe will be waiting in the wings at the nearest parking garage.

I unlock my car and slide into the seat. "It's a free meal and a reason to wear your new Jimmy Choos." I back out of my parking space and laugh at myself for the second time in an hour. From primping like it's prom to giving myself a pep talk just to make it through the night. Pathetic.

I drive downtown to the agreed upon restaurant and choose to park myself rather than use the valet. Giving my keys to a random person would mean I'd have more trouble leaving early if it comes to that. I go to the front door and wait as I told Ryan I would.

A few moments pass before a tall man with blondish hair wearing navy slacks steps onto the sidewalk. He's tall, well-dressed and handsome, just like Ariel described. I smile when he comes closer. Even if this isn't Ryan, it can't hurt to smile at a good-looking guy.

He picks up his pace when we lock eyes and stops a few feet in front of me. "You must be Bianca."

"And that would make you Ryan."

"Yes." He smiles, his teeth the embodiment of a toothpaste commercial. "Shall we?" He holds out his arm.

I loop my arm in his and try not to laugh. Shall we? Were we going to eat dinner or make our mark on society at a debutante ball?

He leads me to the door and opens it but doesn't hold it open. I catch it with my free hand before it smacks my side as he drags me through the opening. A far cry from Jack opening doors and coddling me into a car as if I were a helpless toddler. Suddenly I miss Jack's over-the-top door-openings.

I blink in an effort to rid my brain of all things Jack. At least for tonight. That's why I agreed to this date in the first place, right? Besides, if I can hold my own in other areas, I can hold my own doors.

"Table for two, under Connor." Ryan flashes a flirty smile at the young girl behind the reservation desk.

She returns his smile and blushes. "Yes, right this way." She leads us to a small table in the back corner beside a large window. "Enjoy. Your waiter will be out shortly." She places a menu the size of a children's book in front of each of us, then walks away.

I hang my purse on the edge of my chair and sit down. My eyes gravitate toward the large window that overlooks a small pond with a fountain in the center. Spotlights surrounding the pond reveal giant goldfish milling around and a bridge on the other end. "This is beautiful."

"It sure is." I turn to Ryan's eyes scanning me up and down. It creeps me out a little, and then I realize he wasn't referring to the koi pond.

I open my menu and drop my eyes, hoping he'll do the same. "Have you eaten here before?"

"A few times with some business colleagues."

"Oh." I look up momentarily to not come off as rude. "And what do you do?"

Ryan clears his throat and sips water from the glass in front of him. "I manage a large kitchen and bath supply chain, based here in Atlanta."

"Cool."

"And Ariel works for you?"

I waver my head. "Not really. More like she works with me. She's our HR lady."

"Yeah, but you're like the big boss."

"Nope. That would be my dad." I take a long gulp of water and glance out the window so he won't catch my involuntary eye roll.

Ryan flips through the menu like someone searching for buried treasure. "There." He lands on a page near the back. "The kale and beet salad is amazing."

"Oh. I didn't see that on the salad menu."

"That's because it's on the vegan page."

"There's a vegan page?" I raise an eyebrow. "Well, I guess they've got room for it in here." I laugh nervously.

Ryan reaches across the table and flips my menu to the

same page. I scan over some of the options. It all sounds like something a celebrity would feed to a pet rabbit. I love fresh vegetables as much as anyone, but what's wrong with tossing a little oil on them?

I turn back to the front of the book with dinner choices that cover all the major food groups. About the time I narrow it down to two options, an attractive redhead appears.

"Hello, I'm Lacey, and I'll be your server tonight."

"Well, hello, Lacey. I'm Ryan."

Seriously? Same way he ogled me and the same way he smiled at the hostess, all in one. What was with this dude?

Lacey giggles, and I hide my exasperation behind another huge gulp of water. "Are you two ready to order?"

"I'd like an expert's opinion. What do you recommend, Lacey?" OMG. He bats his eyes at her.

Lacey smiles wider and rattles off the specials, then gives her recommendation for the filet mignon with new potatoes. Ryan hangs on her every word, his smile increasing as she continues. "So, can I interest you in the special?"

"Oh no, I'm a vegan."

I choke, spitting up the water in my mouth. Lacey hands me a stack of napkins, while Ryan leans back and snarls.

"Thank you." I direct my thanks to Lacey as I blot water off my blouse. The last thing I need is to turn this five-star train wreck into a wet T-shirt contest. "And I think I'll have the special. It sounds delicious."

"Beet salad with rye bread for me." Ryan hands our menus to Lacey, wincing at the second-hand water droplets on the edge of mine. Then, he gives Lacey a seductive smirk.

Lacey snatches the menus, ignoring his lingering glare. "All right, I'll go put in your orders. If you two need anything at all, don't hesitate to ask."

"Sure thing, Lacey." Ryan cranes his neck to watch her

leave. I settle back in my seat, focusing on the fish outside. For a split second I wonder if Jack decided to build his pond.

"You eat meat?"

I shift my eyes to Ryan. "Steak and chicken and fish. Nothing exotic or gamey though like . . . venison." The mention of deer sends a shiver up my spine. Jack is probably tossing meat on the grill right now.

"Those are still animals."

"Obviously."

He tilts his head as if he doesn't get sarcasm. Maybe the protein deficiency has affected his brain cells. "And that doesn't bother you?"

I shake my head. "No." I've met my share of people who are vegan, but none of them have tried to shame me out of eating chicken. And some eat that way strictly on the conviction that it will help control their weight.

"Ariel didn't tell me you eat meat." Ryan blinks as if this is a major dealbreaker for him.

"I'm sorry, but I do. And so do Ariel and Toby."

"Yeah, but I'm not on a date with them."

"And you're also not on a date with Lacey."

"What?" His brows furrow with confusion.

How can he not realize that flirting with every woman in sight might just be dealbreaker for the woman he's taken on the date? Except that he didn't take me. I drove myself.

Like magic, Lacey appears with our food. I moisten my lips at the savory steak and new potatoes dripping with olive oil. "Lacey, do you mind bringing me a to-go box?"

"Sure thing." She sets our plates in front of us. An array of red and green shreds, Ryan's looks better suited for a centerpiece at a Christmas charity event than a meal. Lacey grins and turns on her heels. A moment later, she comes back with a large box and a bag to hold it.

"Thank you." I open the box and try not to laugh at

Ryan's gawking. Maybe he'll string his neck so far, it will get stuck.

Once Lacey is out of sight, he turns to me. "So you're one of those women who puts half the food away first to control how much she eats. Smart."

I frown. "Something like that." I stab my steak and move it to the center of the box. Then, I pick up my plate and rake all the potatoes and oily residue into the corner compartments. When I shut the box and stand, Ryan opens his mouth to say something.

But I beat him to it. "Ryan, I would say it's been a pleasure, but it hasn't. So, I'll simply say thanks for dinner." His mouth continues to drop as I swing my purse over my shoulder, snatch up my food, and strut away with my head held high.

When I settle into my car, I peer into the rearview mirror and smile. I got exactly what I expected from this date and nothing more.

A nice meal.

CHAPTER SIXTEEN

Jack

I had survived the arrival of a new group. And Jonah's potato skins were such a hit, I decided to add them to the regular rotation. It helps to have other people around, whether Jonah or guests. Just anybody other than Chocolate and Brownie. As much as I adore those dogs, I need someone to make small talk with me and keep my mind from wandering. And it has wandered a lot over the past week.

Not so much about the land or even my plans for working on a fishing pond in between guest reservations. No, it's Bianca.

I don't want to think about what she might be doing. But I can't help myself. Everywhere I go and everything I do makes me think of her. I can't even drive by the general store without wondering if she's worn her boots since she left. And would she put ice cream on honeybuns from now on? Or find a shooting range in Atlanta to blow off some steam using her newly found gun skills?

I sigh. Probably a negative on all fronts. But maybe she thinks of me from time to time. Otherwise, the amount of time she spends in my mind is all for nothing.

I pick up a piece of bacon with some tongs and shake off the grease before setting it on a plate. Planning to feed eight men for the week, not counting myself, had resulted in my buying all the bacon I could find at the Pig. Maybe I should consider adding hog hunting. Not that I have time to slaughter hogs.

I yawn from having waken up before sunrise. Contrary to my plan, I never made it to the shooting house. Instead, I'd sat on the front porch of my cabin with a dog on each side. And as an hour passed and the sun rose, I tried to justify the emptiness I feel inside.

Maybe once I pay off the lodge I'll have closure and that pit in my stomach will go away. Or if I finish a fishing pond and shooting range to offer more amenities for my guests. Maybe then, the puzzle of my life won't have a missing piece.

The last few strands of bacon pop, and I turn down the heat. I let them cook a few more seconds, then put them on a plate. Not thinking, I grab the skillet handle to move the pan. I quickly let it go when my palm throbs with heat. Man, I miss my fish mitt.

I squeeze my hand into a fist until it stops pulsing, then reach for my backup pot holder to move the pan. That had been the only fish mitt at Paul's store. And it might have been the only one ever made. Too bad it died so young.

Setting the bacon aside, I start on the eggs. I also put some canned biscuits in the oven in case the bacon doesn't carry as far as I hope. I need to save a few packs for the rest of their stay in case Piggly Wiggly doesn't restock in time.

A little later, laughter rings out down the hall, signifying that at least some of the guests are awake. I pull out some plates and forks as I finish the eggs. A few men trickle in and greet me.

"I have eggs and bacon, and biscuits will be ready in a minute." I point to enough bacon and eggs to fill a breakfast buffet, then move out of the way so they can start fixing plates.

I start a pot of coffee as I wait on the biscuits. The coffee and biscuits go off about the same time, so I retrieve both. Then, I go to the refrigerator for butter, milk and creamer.

I stare at the creamer. Bianca picked it out, along with her cappuccino packets. Great. More hints of her existence. I shut the refrigerator door and set the creamer on the counter beside the coffee. I busy myself pulling down mugs and try to forget about her. But the absence of my two ugliest mugs makes that hard to do.

A smile forms across my face as the image of her reacting to the skinned deer plays out in my mind. I laugh a little to myself, then shut the cabinet door.

"Do you guys have everything you need?"

Everyone either nods or mumbles a "yeah, thanks."

"Okay. I'll be outside getting the vehicles ready." I exit through the kitchen door and cross the patio. My feet feel heavy when they land where Bianca stood a week earlier. She'd just gotten off the phone and stared at me with fear and confusion.

Could that phone call be the conversation she thought I'd overheard? I shake my head. It doesn't matter much now.

I continue on to the shop and back out the vehicles. Both of the side-by-sides, as well as my two four-wheelers. I can lead the group on one and let someone else drive the other. And there's no woman this time to distract me.

Somehow, that doesn't exactly lift my spirits.

I pour myself a bowl of cereal and trudge to my recliner. I've just helped send a well-deserving man into retirement with two more bucks to his name. Not to mention all the deer scored by the rest of the guys. And thanks to Mrs. Mary's help in the kitchen, everyone left with a full belly and a smiling face.

I will go back to the lodge tomorrow and clean all the rooms. After wiping down the kitchen, all I'd wanted was to go home and take a shower. And the eight hungry men hadn't left a stitch of leftovers from lunch. That meant cereal for dinner.

Brownie wags over to me, and I point to the ground for her to sit. I need a few uninterrupted minutes to feed myself instead of everyone else—people and animals alike. The dog obeys, and I bow my head for a quick prayer.

After saying "amen," I lift my head and scoop a spoonful of cereal into my mouth. I reach for the TV remote but change my mind. I don't need to get sucked into a show, tired as I am. Once this bowl of cereal disappears, I plan on calling it a night.

Halfway into finishing my Frosted Flakes, someone knocks on the front door. I sigh and set my cereal bowl on the end table. I point to Brownie and then to my eyes to warn her not to take advantage of within-reach food.

I open the door just enough to peek through a crack since I'm in my boxer briefs. A deer stares me in the eye. I blink. Have I officially gone crazy, or have the deer gotten smart enough to knock?

The door swings open, and Roy's head pops out from behind the deer. "So, what do ya think?" He glances down at my camo boxers. "Whoa, sorry, man."

I shake my head, then focus back on the deer. I rub my

chin as I examine it closer. It's Bianca's deer. The one I'd asked Roy to fully mount. How could I forget? "Let me just say it looks so real, Roy, that you fooled me for a moment."

"I know, right? I took a bunch of photos of this beauty." Roy laughs and slaps the backside of the deer. It rolls toward me, and I notice he's put it on wheels. Clever. "Do you mind if I put him on my website?"

I scrunch my brow. "You have a website?"

"Of course, I do. Everyone has a website, Jack."

I nod. "I suppose they do."

"I knew I'd find ya here, but I'll be glad to take him up to the big house. Shouldn't be that hard seeing as how I put him on wheels and all."

I run a hand across my still-wet hair and shrug. "It's fine. I can move it later."

"You sure?"

"Yeah, Roy."

"All right." Roy smirks and cups his hand around the bill of his Remington cap. "Thanks again."

"Sure thing, Roy." I roll the deer inside and shut the door behind me. I lean against the wall and stare at it until I hear Roy's truck pull away.

Glaring into the eyes of that deer brings back too many memories. Why didn't I have Roy take it on to the lodge? Because that would mean I'd have to go unlock the lodge, and to do that, I'd need to get up and put on clothes. That's why.

But now I realize my mistake. That deer can't stay here. Not in my house. One of two things will happen. Either the dogs will end up chewing on its legs, or I'll end up shooting it in the head. On second thought, maybe I should keep it here.

Nope. This job cost way too much to ruin. At the time I'd commissioned Roy to do it, I planned on giving it to

Bianca as a gift. Luckily, I saw her true colors before Roy completed the job. Just not before I'd written him a fat check.

Now I'm stuck with an equally fat animal statue. My house is too small to hide it. I slap my forehead and groan. I know what I have to do.

Not caring to fully dress, I grab the pair of boots I keep close to the door and pull them over my bare feet. Then, I go to the hall closet and throw on a coat and my trusty headlamp. Armed and ready, I go back to the door and wheel the beast onto the porch.

I walk backwards down the front porch steps, easing the deer down behind me. Every tug reminds me how heavy the thing is. But after four steps, we're on solid ground.

Roy has vans with gates and pulleys. I have none of that. But I do have lifts. So I push the buck toward the shop and loop a rope around its neck, lasso style, then secure it to the lift on my side-by-side. I tie it more securely after raising it off the ground.

The legs hang stiff, as to be expected from any petrified object. It should be fine as long as I don't back into anything.

I creep up the drive and park by the back patio. Then, I cut the engine and untie the deer. When I do, the legs tip off the lift and the deer goes rolling down the backyard hill. I rush after it and catch it mid-way down. Only one tine is chipped on the antler.

I sigh. Why am I protecting this deer? Other than making an impressive decoration in the lodge, what will it ever bring me besides heartache? The woman who killed it also killed my heart.

That's when I get an idea. I'll make it a moving target. I roll it back toward the dirt pile and park it in front of the bank, not caring if it somehow scoots away.

Then, I drive home and fall asleep without the dead deer there to haunt me.

⚞ ⚟

Bianca

I turn up the volume on my phone. My ears vibrate as pop music pulses through my earbuds. Anything to drown out my thoughts. Even at the cost of losing half my hearing.

I round the block, my feet beating the pavement like cinderblocks. The neighborhood playground rises over the hill, and I push myself to make it there. Then, I collapse on the first bench I come to and throw my head back.

My heart pounds as I pause my music. Running used to calm my worries. A bad date? Go for a run. Business deal gone wrong? Run harder. Disagreement with a parent or friend? Run like my life depends on it. And after a few miles, my mind—and my body—thanks me for the refresher.

But running doesn't work when it comes to Jack. And neither does anything else. Not dating other men, buying new clothes, burying myself in work, or even traveling. I just got back from Charleston, one of my favorite low-key cities. The client is a clothing designer, and I woke up early each morning to walk in the historic districts. Yet, none of it made me happy.

Something's wrong.

Ever since I came home from Apple Cart, things haven't been the same. I'm different. Jaded. Even more cynical than before. Which, for me, is saying a lot.

I blink at the sun beating down on me and breathe in the

crisp air. What made me a nervous wreck? Not getting Jack to sell his land? Or simply not getting Jack? Perhaps both.

Macon and Ronald seem happy, moving right along with the stores in other states. And focusing on them plus other clients in various stages of growth has kept me plenty busy. And after my date with Toby's golf buddy turned into a dumpster fire, I even considered texting William, an old acquaintance who'd hinted on more than one occasion that he'd like to take me to dinner. But whatever is going on with me, work or love-related, I have to admit that William isn't the answer. Apparently, neither is running.

I stand and stretch my legs before turning in the direction of my apartment. The cool air refreshes my face as I jog home. I slow down as I approach my building. My breathing calms by the time I'm on the elevator. Maybe after a hot shower and some green tea, I can relax.

That is only wishful thinking. Once in my apartment, I barely have time to shower and pull on a pair of lounge pants when my doorbell rings. "Who is it?" I yell from the bedroom, not wanting to answer unless necessary.

"Mom. Are you home?"

"Yeah, be there in a sec." I jerk a T-shirt over my head and hurry to the door. "Hi, Mom."

"Hey, baby. I want to talk to you about something." She smiles, but something sad lingers in her green eyes.

"Okay." I open the door wider and motion for her to come inside. It isn't like her to not just call first, which means this talk will hold more weight than our usual conversations.

"Is Dad okay?"

She wavers her head and drops her gaze.

My limbs tingle as I follow her into the living room. "I've told him to watch what he eats. His cholesterol isn't something to play around with."

"It's not that." She eases onto the couch and sweeps her

blond bangs to the side. "It's us." She stares at me, a few tears pooling in her eyes.

I sit beside her and take her hand. "I didn't realize things were bad until the other night."

"What happened the other night?" She sniffles.

"I called Dad about work and asked if you were home." I shrug. "I just wanted to say hi, but he said you hadn't been home in weeks. And since we'd met in town a few times, I knew it wasn't because you'd been on a long trip."

She reaches out and strokes my cheek. "My smart girl. Nothing gets past you."

I let out a sarcastic laugh and tilt my head to let Mom's hand fall from my face. "You'd be surprised." If nothing got past me, I'd have picked up on what bothered Jack.

"I love your father, I really do. But I'm not sure he loves me."

"Mom. How can you say that?" I stare at my bare feet, not completely convinced Mom isn't right.

"Let me rephrase that. I'm not sure your dad loves me more than he loves work."

I push my back into the couch cushions and sigh. I can't refute that statement. "I think we could all say that."

Mom gives me a pitying stare. "Your father loves you more than anyone."

"Maybe anyone. But anything?" I clench my teeth. Deep down, I know he puts work before everything. And, if he would admit it, he could trace that back to the reason behind having two failed marriages and not much of a relationship with his oldest daughters.

Mom says nothing and blots away tears with her fingertips. Both of us admitting out loud how much work means to Dad simultaneously lifts a weight off my shoulders and clamps a chain around my ankle. Do I dare confront Dad about his priorities? And do I even have a right to do so, given how much I work?

"You know," I pause to blink back my own tears. "Dad said I'm just like him."

"No, baby. You're not."

"Are you sure?" I ask mainly because if anyone would build me up, it would be Mom. When she doesn't respond, I continue. "I've pretty much set aside everything in the name of a deal, costing me time, friends, and love."

Yes, love. The word leaves my lips numb, but I mean it. I love Jack. Sure, I've only spent a few days with him, but it turned into one of the best weeks of my life. What other explanation could I have for living in a fog ever since I left Alabama?

"Baby, if this is about choosing college over Rich?" Concern clouds Mom's face.

I giggle. "No, Mom. Not even close."

"Do you want to talk about it?" She reaches for my hand and gives it a squeeze.

I consider her offer. I need to talk to someone before I explode. And Ariel will only try and slap another Band-Aid of a man on my wounded heart. I nod. "I do." I squeeze Mom's hand back, then stand. "But first I need to sear some honeybuns."

CHAPTER SEVENTEEN

Jack

"Thank you. I look forward to your visit as well. Goodbye." I hang up the phone and smile. That's the third corporate meeting I've booked this week, and I know exactly who to thank.

Macon and Ronald each left individual reviews on my website, praising both me and the lodge. But what really brought Gamer's Paradise attention was Macon's mention of it in a national wilderness magazine. *All Things Wilderness* had interviewed Macon about his stores expanding into the Southeastern region. He mentioned holding the business meeting at Gamer's Paradise and complimented my lodge and hospitality. But the real kicker was when he'd described the size of the bucks he and Ronald killed and how I had the meat packaged and the busts ready to mount by the time they left.

These three upcoming meetings would make for a nice

transition into springtime and hopefully pay for my time building a pond. Then, I could offer fishing after the seasons end.

I sink back into my couch and scroll through my contacts. I press Macon's cell number. It rings a few times, then he answers. "Hello, Jack."

"Hi, Macon. How are you?"

"I'm great. How have you been? It's so good to hear from you."

I can practically hear his smile. I imagine many people tell him "pleasure doing business with you" and actually mean it.

"I'm good. Real good, thanks to you and Ronald." Now I can hear my own smile. "I wanted to call and thank you guys for the reviews on my site and especially for you mentioning me in the magazine story."

"Oh, Jack. No thanks necessary. All I did was state my honest opinion." Regardless of what he says, I know good and well he graciously said more than needed to answer a simple question.

"Well, anytime you and Ronald want to come back for free, just let me know."

"That's really generous of you, but I can't stay for free."

"Then how about you let me keep the meat of whatever you kill, and we call it even?"

"We'll kill it, and you cook it. Sounds like a good deal." We both laugh. "You know, I'll be coming through Alabama again in a few days."

"Really? What part?"

"That depends." He takes a long pause before continuing. "Bianca narrowed it down to two options to locate the new store, and I'm trying to decide. One's in the northern part of the state and the other is near the Gulf Coast."

My mouth goes dry. For the past few weeks, I've prayed

and thought about my decision with the land. Even considered putting the back acreage up for sale. I confided in Jonah about my reservations but realized that I need to pay down the lodge before moving on with other projects. I stand and pace the length of my living room, trying to work up the courage to ask. The dogs lay in the corner in their beds, moving their heads with my steps like they're being hypnotized. They probably think I'm crazy. And maybe I am. Ah, heck. It's now or never.

"Macon, how serious were you about buying some of my land when Bianca mentioned it?" There I said it.

"Well, Jack. Your land was always my number one pick."

I open my mouth to respond, but my jaw locks. I stand frozen with the phone to my ear.

"Jack, are you still there?"

I blink. "Yes, I . . . I'd love to come and talk with you about it sometime."

"How about next Thursday when I plan on coming to Alabama."

I start seeing spots like those old cartoons where they get hit in the head with a mallet. This is really happening. "Yeah, absolutely."

"Okay, I'll email you the details once I finalize my plans."

"Sounds great. I'll be sure to hold a room for you."

"Perfect. Talk to you soon."

"Yes, sir." I hold the phone to my ear for a moment after Macon hangs up. I stand there with what I'm sure is a stupid smile on my face. Then one of the dogs barks. I put my phone in my overalls pocket, then pat both my legs. The dogs rush over and jump on me. Still weak from the shock of what just happened, I fall back. I laugh as Chocolate and Brownie take advantage of having me on their level by licking my face. Any other time, I'd back them off. But if all goes well, in a matter of a few days, I could be down fifty acres and up a lot of money.

Bianca

I hear a knock on my office door. I take a sip of my cappuccino before answering. "Come in."

Ariel trots in with some file folders in her hands. "Some updates came in on a few of your clients."

"Thanks." I take the folders and shuffle through them, pausing when I notice Outdoorsmen Oasis on a tab. I didn't expect any updates from them this week.

"You still good to grab lunch later?"

I raise my eyes. With my full attention on the folder, I didn't realize Ariel is still standing there. "Yeah, noon?"

"Sounds good. There's this new guy I want to tell you about."

I roll my eyes so far back in my head that I can't see. "Ariel."

"Come on, Bianca. He's nothing like that sleaze Ryan, I promise. I met him at church."

I toss the files on my desk and run my hands down my face. "Ariel, not all guys at church are dateable."

"What's that supposed to mean?" She frowns.

I cross my arms. "Let's just say some are single for a season, and others are single for a reason."

She giggles. "That's too funny. I've never heard that before."

"Well, I have." I widen my eyes, recalling some of the "for a reason" guys I've met.

"Okay, fine. We'll just grab chicken salad and talk about boring things like our jobs and gym classes."

"That's my girl." I smirk.

Ariel shakes her head, then flips her dark hair over her shoulder and trots away.

I rub my temples and pick up the Outdoorsmen Oasis file. I open it to the first page, which gives an overview of the update. "Land confirmed for new Alabama store location." I turn the page, anxious to see which site Macon and Ronald have chosen.

I read "Jack Jackson, Apple Cart, Alabama" as the seller. I drop the folder and fling my hands over my mouth, knocking my coffee cup back. Cameral-colored liquid floods my white silk blouse, stinging my chest with its heat.

I leap to my feet and hold out my shirt, trying to peel it away from my skin. My bra peeks through like I'm trying to look trendy in one of those sheer shirts. Except I'm not. I'm a professional. Oh, and I have a huge brown mess on me. Crap. As if this isn't bad enough, I have nothing else to wear except my gym clothes. I'll need to run home and change.

Once the liquid cools, I pull my keyring from my purse. I hug my arms across my chest and crouch as I rush to the hallway restroom a few doors down from my office. I stuff paper towels in my shirt to both separate it from my skin and keep everything from looking so transparent. I hear a toilet flush, signaling I'm not alone. Ms. Abbot, an older secretary, comes out of the center stall and glares at me. I smile as I shove paper towels up my shirt. She shakes her head and washes her hands.

I try to act casual, which is hard when you have one hand up your shirt and the other ripping paper towels out of the dispenser like an amateur magician pulling handkerchiefs from his hand. Ms. Abbot clears her throat. I move to the side so she can get a paper towel. She frowns at me, then wipes her hands and leaves.

Once I've stuffed enough paper towels in my shirt to camouflage my bra, I step back and examine my work in the mirror. I turn to the side. Hmm. So this is what it's like to have double-Ds. I pat my chest. Well, real ones wouldn't be so lumpy. I see a note on one of the stall doors in the mirror. I go snatch it off and hold it at chest level. That helps to hide the brown. Wait. I flip it around so that I'm not a walking billboard for "Don't flush feminine products."

So, with a shirt stuffed more than a mall Santa's and hugging a backwards sign to my chest, I make my way to the elevators. I panic when I come to the stairwell door and opt for the long way down. I keep the paper to my chest in case I meet someone on the way to my car. After twelve flights of stairs, I open the exit door to the parking lot. The sun blasts my vision. I feel like someone getting out of prison for the first time.

I speed-walk across the parking lot, my feet cursing me for making them take the stairs in stilettos. I'm almost to my car when my secretary rushes across the parking lot.

"Bianca!"

I debate getting in my car and peeling out as if I haven't heard her. But I've already turned around. I freeze and let her come to me. I've already littered a few pieces of paper towels on the way down. No need to drop more.

"Bianca, there you are. Your dad is looking for you everywhere. He wants you to call him ASAP."

"Is everything okay?"

"There's a client you need to meet with."

I groan. "Thanks, Cindy." I unlock my car and exchange the bathroom warning sign for my gym bag. I hug it close to my chest and follow Cindy back inside. We take the elevator together, since I have a better shield now. I'm sure Cindy is curious as to why I'm hugging a duffle bag like someone would an oversized stuffed animal won at a fair instead of carrying it by the shoulder straps. Or why I have a duffle bag at all. But who cares.

I rush to my office and lock the door behind me. I unzip my bag and pull out the bra and shirt I'd packed. I peel off my sticky blouse and bra, as paper towels litter the floor like dirty snowballs. I put on my sports bra and tank top in record time. Now I can at least stay dry until I talk to Dad. Then, I'll run home to change.

I buzz Dad's phone. "Dad."

"There's a client here to meet with you." No hello or anything, just right to it.

"Now?" I stare down at my black pencil skirt and faded tank top with "cardio queen" screen printed across the boobs. Wonderful. Party on the top and business on the bottom.

"Uh, can't it wait until after lunch? I'm really busy."

"No, when someone comes to meet with you and you're here, you drop what you're doing and meet with them. Get to the conference room."

"Okay . . ." Uh. If it was anyone but Dad, I'd try to explain. But he won't accept any excuses when it comes to a client. I hang up the intercom and bang my head against the wall. Ariel. Where is Ariel? We're about the same size.

Not caring to grab a shield this time, I rush out of my office toward Ariel's desk. "Ariel, I need the shirt off your back."

She squints my way. "Cardio queen? That's a new one."

"No, I spilt cappuccino on myself, and this was in my gym bag."

"What color is your bra?"

"What?" I shake my head. "What does that matter?

"Well, I'm wearing a light pink blouse with a blush

colored bra. You're wearing a maroon tank top and the straps under it look black." She points to my shoulder.

I have on a black sports bra. I slap my forehead. "So I can wear a shirt that shows my sports bra or be cardio queen, right?"

Ariel nods. "Afraid so."

I drum my fingers on Ariel's desk. "Wait, did you bring a sweater today?"

"Of course not. You know your dad keeps this place eighty-five degrees in the winter."

"Fine, thanks." I rush to the conference room, prepared to introduce my client to the cardio queen. Not that I'll be able to focus on this meeting anyway, knowing that Jack has decided to sell his land.

Jack

I push more dirt into my pile and back up the bulldozer. Thanks to the sale of the land, I'm able to pay off the mortgage on the lodge. That frees up cash to rent equipment and start on the pond. Whatever dirt I dig up from the pond, I'll use to create the shooting range. Everything is going according to plan.

I always leave at least a day between guests to clean up everything, double-check the deer feeders, and gas up all the vehicles. Instead of going home to relax after I clean, I've been going straight to the pond to work. I've barely had time to sleep.

More than a month has passed since I've seen Bianca, and I'm sure she knows I sold my land to the store. I scratch my whiskered chin and wonder what she thinks of that. Guilt rumbles inside of me as I recall the conversations we had about the land. I'd scolded her for suggesting I do such a thing. Then, I went and did it anyway without her.

She must think I'm the most selfish hypocrite in the world.

If I could go back in time, I would have remained calmer and weighed my options instead of jumping to conclusions. But time only travels one way, and it's not backwards. I back up for more dirt and try not to dwell on what I've done wrong.

Instead, I dwell on whether I'll ever meet another woman who makes me feel the way Bianca did. Or if I'll ever allow myself to get that close to a woman again. Was the risk really worth the reward?

A lot guys my age are married now. Some even have kids. But I have Tanner and Jonah. That is, until they decide to start their own families. Then, where will that leave me? Meeting all the widowers at Mrs. Mary's for a five a.m. cup of coffee and going to bed with the sun?

I remove my cap and rake my fingers through my hair. I need a haircut. And I need to shave. Not that I have anyone to impress, but even I've grown tired of my scruffiness.

I check the time on my phone. New guests will come soon, so I'd best park the bulldozer for now. I've accomplished a lot for a Sunday afternoon.

I drop the bulldozer key in the pocket of my overalls and drive my truck back to the lodge. No sooner than I've straightened a few things around the living room, two trucks park out front.

I go outside to welcome them. This week's guests are fathers and sons, which is always fun. It reminds me of when Jonah and I would hunt with our dads and Grandpa. Two dads and two kids emerge from each vehicle. I shake their hands and formally introduce myself. It doesn't take but a second for the youngest boy to run through the yard toward the back.

"Son, don't run off," one of the men calls after him.

"He's fine. Nothing back there that can hurt him," I assure.

"I'm more worried about what he can hurt." The man laughs, and so do the rest of us.

I lead everyone around back, talking about the patio and the cell service as we pass by. When we round the house, I notice the boy standing down by the dirt pile staring at something.

I walk everyone down the back yard and explain that we're going to the shooting range where they can test their guns. The little boy rushes over to us as we come closer. I smile down at him. "What did you find?"

"A deer. On roller-skates." He smiles, revealing several missing teeth.

"Those are just wheels to move it around."

"Wow, cool." He rushes back to Bianca's deer. He reaches down and touches the wheels.

"Careful, Justin," his dad calls out and starts walking toward the dirt mound. I follow.

"I've never seen a real dead deer that can stand."

I laugh. "I had him mounted like that."

"Oh. Why?" Justin snarls his nose.

"Because it's a special deer."

"Then why is it by all this dirt?"

"Because we shoot at it."

He frowns and stokes the deer's face. "If I had something this special, I wouldn't keep shooting it. I'd put it in my room and never let it go."

I swallow. I've taken out all my frustration on Bianca's deer. All because I was so stupid as to let her go. I squat down by the boy. "That's a good idea, Justin. Would you like to help me roll it inside?"

Bianca

I hum to myself as I fold shirts into my turquoise suitcase. I close it and shrug on the leather jacket I purchased a few weeks ago when I booked this trip. I check my hair in the mirror and smirk at my midnight shimmer manicure and dark jacket.

For all that went wrong for me in Alabama, I did gain a sense of adventure. So, when Dad asked for someone to meet with a bike shop owner in Chicago, I volunteered right away. Besides, if I can kill a buck, I can possibly ride a bike. Maybe even drive one.

I'll just steer clear of any hot biker dudes.

That should be easy enough since bike shops don't offer onsite accommodations. And since I still can't seem to shake Jack from my mind. It's all I can do to keep him from moving into my heart as well.

I'll get over him one day, as I have everything else in life. My failed teen marriage, bad business deals, and the time that garbage truck driver backed over my Mercedes. Besides, if I can book a new client with "cardio queen" written across my chest, I can manage to climb out of any valley life leads me through.

And like any uphill battle, the harder I climb, the farther it will push Jack into my distant memory. At least, that's my hope.

I set my luggage on the floor and retrieve my shoe bag

from the closet. Then, I reach against the back wall for my tall black boots. When I do, my hand brushes against soft leather. I grab the square toe and pull out a cowgirl boot. So much for pushing back Jack.

The day I bought those boots floods my memory. More boots than I could count lined the back wall of that oddball store. And I couldn't concentrate for all the funeral flowers and curtain rods poking me as I walked around. Then, Jack spotted the most perfect pair of boots for me.

I run my hand down the embroidered leg of the boot before pushing it to the back of my closet. I intend to leave it there, but my hand misbehaves by pulling it back out, along with its twin.

Staring down at the pair conjures up a mix of emotions. I twist my lips. What should I do with these? Throw them in the closet before my hand goes rogue again? Donate them to charity? Or . . . I kick off my black booties and tug the turquoise boots over my skinny jeans. I stand in front of my floor-length mirror and turn, taking in every angle of those majestic shoes.

Something jerks at my heart when I lift my eyes to take in my overall appearance. I wish Jack could see me dressed like this. If for no other reason than for me to see him.

My shoulders droop, and I sigh heavily. I leave the mirror in favor of my bed and plop back, staring at the ceiling fan. I've spent the last week fighting the urge to pry to Macon about the land sale. Not so much because it matters to me where he builds the store. But I can't for the life of me understand why Jack had a sudden change of heart.

Especially after he had a sudden change of heart about *me* over the same thing.

CHAPTER EIGHTEEN

Jack

I drum my thumbs on the steering wheel, anxious to finally be on this trip. For the last four days, I've cantered around the lodge like a ticking time bomb. Father and son hunts are my favorite to host, especially when at least one son on the hunt has never killed a deer before. As I suspected, this last group's rookie was the snaggle-toothed kid who'd commented on Bianca's deer on roller skates.

Little Justin left with his first deer and a grin so wide that all the soap in Alabama couldn't have washed it off. But in all honestly, I've never been so ready to see my guests go. Not that I didn't enjoy them. Quite the opposite. But I was itching to go myself.

I slow my truck as another light turns red in front of me. I'll never understand why anyone would choose to live in Atlanta. I can count on one hand how many times I've been here before. And this makes the only time I didn't come to watch a Brave's game.

If Bianca doesn't know how much I care about her, she will before I leave. Whether she reciprocates those feelings is totally up to her. But I'll sure give us a fighting chance.

As traffic squeezes around me on an overpass, I pull up my location app and search for Manderson Money Management. The pinpoint appears. Less than ten miles from where I am now. Of course, that might take an hour, at the rate I'm going.

I white-knuckle my steering wheel and clench my stomach. A ball of nerves ping-pongs inside my gut as scenarios play out in my mind. What if she throws me out and never wants to speak to me again? Or worse, what if she refuses to speak to me at all?

I'm pretty sure she knows about the land sale, but I'm not certain. Will she be mad at me for blowing up on her about it, then selling? Or will she glory in her victory of knowing best? I puff up my cheeks, then exhale. Maybe it all depends on her personal feelings for me.

If she cares for me even half as much as I do her, then she'll celebrate the sale. On the flip side, if all she ever wanted from me was to please her business clients, then she may balk at me for refusing to sell when it was her idea.

A horn honks behind me, jolting me back to attention. I roll my truck the few yards the car in front of me has moved and then return my feet to the brake and clutch. So that's why city people don't know how to drive stick shifts. Half an hour of this stop and go, and my left leg has already started cramping.

I move another few feet when I notice blue lights up ahead. The vehicle in front of me turns on its right blinker and changes lanes when another lets it in. I do the same. I idle my truck in the right lane for a few minutes before seeing three wrecked cars and a ton of rubberneckers on the bridge. Once I make it past the wreck, I sail through downtown at a decent speed.

A dozen traffic lights later, my phone directs me to turn. I take a left onto a side street that leads me to a large skyscraper. I park in the nearest parking space I can find and feed the meter. Then, I check the bed of my truck to make sure my ratchet straps are secure. I'll come back for the gift after assessing her mood.

I take off my cap and smooth down my hair. I stopped by the hair salon yesterday and shamelessly flirted with Adrianne Reynolds so that she'd cut my hair last minute. And if this doesn't work out with Bianca, I owe Adrianne dinner. But if it does, I'll pay for Tanner or Jonah to treat her.

The height of the building makes my lodge look like a Lego in comparison. I stand at the entrance and crane my head until my neck creaks, and I still can't see the top. I swallow my nerves and head inside.

I can almost see straight through the reflective flooring leading up to a large desk. "Hi, ma'am. I'm looking for the office of Manderson Money Management."

A middle-aged woman dressed better than anyone from Apple Cart in her Sunday best cuts her eyes toward me. "Floor twelve. Suite 1201."

"Thank you."

She says nothing, just drops her eyes and continues typing on her computer. I decide I'd best find the elevators on my own rather than disturb her further.

I ride the elevator up to the twelfth floor, as instructed. The doors open three times on the way up, and each time I debate getting out. But no, I've come here for a reason. And I deserve closure from Bianca, if for no other reason than burning four hours of diesel fuel.

At last, the number twelve lights up above my head and

the doors open. "Excuse me." I step past the two people in front of me and onto the slick surface of the hallway. A sign with the suite numbers points me to the right.

I walk down a long hallway and open the door with Manderson Money Management stamped across it in gold. Fancy. Not that I expected anything less. I hold my breath and thrust myself inside. I cross the floor to the desk at the end of the room. "Hi." My voice comes out squeaky, so I clear my throat. "Is Bianca Manderson here?"

"I don't think so." The young woman at the desk runs a finger across her computer mouse, obviously checking something. She gazes up at me. "One second." I wait as she walks to the open hallway behind her. "Hey, Ariel? Did Bianca come in before her flight?" My heart pounds as I wait for an answer. I can't hear whatever whoever Ariel is says. "There's a guy here asking."

A split second later, a pretty dark-haired woman appears. "Hi, there." She runs her eyes up and down, assessing me, then holds out a hand. "I'm Ariel, HR and Bianca's bestie."

I take her hand, surprised at the firmness of her handshake. The ten-pound diamond on her finger must've build up some great gripping muscles. "I'm Jack Jackson."

Her eyes bug. "Oh. She's not here. I'm so sorry."

My face falls. "Is she on a trip?"

Ariel glances down at her smart watch and taps the screen. "She's at the airport, but you might can catch her there."

"Okay, what airport, where do I go? What gate?" My chest rises and falls as I spill out the questions.

"Hold on, cowboy. I can take you."

"I appreciate that, but I have a gift for her in my truck."

"Well, you can put it in my car." Ariel smiles.

"With all due respect, ma'am, I don't think you have room in your trunk for a dead body."

If I could've bottled the looks on those women's faces when I mentioned a dead body, I'd be rich. I'd market it as "deer in the headlights" scentless cologne and sell it at Outdoorsmen Oasis. I might even give Daisy a cut if she turned it into a candle.

Of course, I quickly clarified that statement by adding "a dead stuffed deer." And without a minute to spare, as the young secretary had placed her hand on the phone. Most likely to call security.

But once they quit gawking at me like I am an axe murderer, Ariel offered to ride along and help me navigate the Atlanta airport. And thank the Good Lord for that. I've flown exactly once in my life. For a hunting trip to Colorado with Dad, Grandpa, Uncle Jeremy, and Jonah. Besides, I was a teenager then, so I simply played on my phone as I followed Dad around.

Ariel points out side streets, directing me to ignore my app's voiceover and follow her lead. I do as I'm told, even if weaving a Dodge Ram through Atlanta traffic feels like trying to squeeze a full deer through a meat processor.

"So you're the dude who owns the hunting mansion?" Ariel asks in between spouting out instructions.

"I guess that's one way you can put it."

"Well, you did quite the number on my friend. She hasn't been the same since she got back from Alabama."

I tighten my grip on the gearshift and breathe heavily. I need this woman's help if I want a fighting chance at catching Bianca before her flight. Sarcasm won't serve me well right now.

"Yeah, I'm here to try to remedy that."

"Oh, I figured as much." Ariel tilts her head. "Take a right on this next street."

I flip on my blinker and shift gears.

"But what's the deal with the stuffed deer on skates?"

"They're not." I frown. Maybe they are skates. Everyone, except for Roy and me, seems to think so. Actually, I've never asked Roy. Maybe he'd intended them to be skates.

"You were saying?"

"Oh yeah. Bianca shot that deer, so I had it stuffed as a gift to her." I glance at Ariel.

She wrinkles her nose, then straightens it as her bright red lips curve into a smile. "That's either the grossest or sweetest thing I've ever heard. Maybe both."

"Thanks?" I slow at a stop sign, then continue on.

"Two more blocks, then we get back on the main interstate. The airport will be about a mile from there."

I nod, then gaze down at my app. "Rerouting" flashes across the map in huge red letters. And had I not muted it a few miles back, the voice would still be repeating it.

Sure enough, as soon as I merge onto the highway, a sign appears for the airport exit. I stay in the right lane and drum my thumbs on the steering wheel.

"You're nervous."

I cut my eyes toward her. "Yeah, wouldn't you be?"

She shrugs. "I've known Bianca since kindergarten, so nothing she could say would intimidate me."

I laugh. "You're probably one of the only ones who can say that."

"Nah. She puts up a tough front, what with the whole woman in a man's working world cliché. But she's one of the most genuine people, once you get to know her."

I had thought the same, for a while. Then, she schmoozed Macon and Ronald behind my back. Of course, the land worked out in their favor—and mine—in the end. But at the time, Bianca playing both sides gave me major trust issues.

I don't care to share any of that with Ariel, especially having no idea what Bianca's shared with her. So I simply smile and keep driving.

I park as convenient to the airport entrance as possible while not wasting any time. I hop out of the truck and untie the deer. Ariel steps out and stares as I drag it off the truck bed, letting its wheels hit the pavement.

"You're taking that in the airport?"

"Why not?"

Ariel clenches her teeth and shrugs. "Well, I've seen crazier around here."

I shut the tailgate and start jogging in the direction of the entrance. Holding my keys over my shoulder, I hit the lock button. Ariel scurries beside me, trying to keep up.

We enter the glass doors, drawing wandering eyes to the deer. People from all cultures scan the animal as if it is a UFO. For some, maybe it is. I'm not well versed in the wildlife of other countries.

As we head toward security, Ariel shoves her phone in my face. "Here."

I stare at the pink rectangle, then at her. "What?"

She shakes it in my face. "Take it. I bought you a ticket so you can get in."

"Oh, thanks." I smile and take the phone, glittery case and all. Then, I march toward the security entrance rolling a dead deer with one hand and palming a pink phone with the other. Not my best look.

A large woman who looks like she's sucked a lemon for lunch spreads her arms across the walkway. "No sir. That beast ain't coming up in here."

Sweat rolls down my neck, as I stroke the deer's back. I have two choices: sell her on true love or fake insanity. For time's sake, I choose the latter. "Ma'am, this is my security deer, Tanner."

"Security deer?" She huffs before letting out a deep belly laugh.

I turn back to see Ariel's eyes widened, as she is witnessing the entire scene. But, since I got the woman's face to unsour, I continue. "Yes, Tanner. He goes everywhere with me. I bought a seat just for him."

She frowns and pulls me to the side so that the other guard can check the impatient people behind me. Then, she holds out her palm and waves her fingers. "Lemme see." I hand her Ariel's phone. She stares at the screen, then narrows her eyes at me. "There's only one ticket on here."

"Yes, that's because Tanner flies alone."

"Pardon me?"

"Tanner flies alone, and I come later. The security is in me knowing he will be there waiting on me."

"That makes no sense."

I drop my shoulders and lower my voice. "Ma'am, have you ever been afraid for all your family to fly together? You know, so in case the plane goes down you don't lose everyone dear to you?" I bite back a smirk at the irony of saying "dear."

Her brown eyes soften. "That thought has crossed my mind."

"Then, you understand why I need to escort Tanner to the terminal."

She puts her hand on my shoulder and sighs. "I guess so. But Tanner will need to go through the scanner."

I nod and smile. I follow her back to a body scanner and catch a glimpse of Ariel out of the corner of my eye. I wink at her, and she shakes her head in disbelief before giving me a thumbs up.

The guards scan "Tanner" for hidden weapons after seeing the bullet holes. I assure them he contains nothing but shreds of lead and stuffing. Then, I embellish my story by saying I rescued him from a gun show exhibit in rural Alabama. That somehow satisfies them, and they even apologize for chipping an antler when shoving him through the scanner.

At last, we make it to the terminal for Bianca's flight.

"Last call for flight 458." A woman's voice calls from the microphone. I frantically scan the space for Bianca. How many tall blonds live in Atlanta, anyway? Apparently, they outnumber the deer in Alabama.

Then, my eyes land on turquoise cowgirl boots. I follow them up to jeans, a leather jacket, and blond ponytail. It has to be her. Who else around here owns a pair of those boots? I rush over, pulling the deer alongside me.

"Sir. I'm afraid you can't board with that, uh, animal. You'll have to check it."

I ignore the woman working the ticket check. "Bianca." She turns her head to the side, then back, as if she isn't sure if she's heard someone call her name. I yell it this time. "Bianca Manderson!"

"Sir!" The woman calls after me. I hug the deer and pray for Bianca to turn around.

She twists her entire upper body and locks eyes with me. Her mouth parts as if she isn't sure how to answer. Her face grows pale. Then, she turns around and continues walking.

But I refuse to let her go without a fight. I slide over to a nearby desk and jerk the microphone closer. "Bianca Manderson. I love you."

With one foot inside the boarding deck, she freezes. Some people look irritated, and others look interested. And the woman bugging me has stopped vying for my attention. People push past Bianca, knocking her side with their carryons, but she doesn't move. So I continue.

"I said I love you, and I was wrong for getting so mad about the land. You were right. I understand if you don't feel the same way about me. But I had to tell you that." My head spins as Bianca boards the plane without looking back. I stand there for what feels like forever, until the ticket woman pulls the mic back toward her and offers me a sympathetic face.

I could move concrete easier than my feet as I trudge between the rows of seats to the exit. Bianca has certainly found her seat by now, and I can't stay any longer waiting for someone who won't come. I leave the terminal and rest against a wall with my arm propped on the deer's back. Ariel walks up beside me and pats my shoulder.

I blink back a tear. "I'll reimburse you for the ticket."

She gives me a compassionate grin. "It's okay. I charged it to the company. Either way, I assumed Bianca should pay for it."

I laugh. Since she'd allowed me to confess my undying love in the middle of the airport while rolling around a shot up deer like a lunatic, I don't much mind her footing the bill.

CHAPTER NINETEEN

Bianca

My hands tremble as I attempt to buckle my seatbelt. Plane seatbelts always cause problems, but today my struggle is more mental than mechanical. I swallow the dry lump in my throat as a tear rolls down my cheek.

I expect to find all kinds of oddities at an international airport. But nothing could've prepared me for Jack dragging around a deer. I'd stood there, my hand on the jetway doorway, fighting the push and pull of whether to run into his arms. I'd heard him plead his case, confess his faults, and even admit I was right.

And I'd heard him profess his love for me.

All the while, I'd glued myself to the floor, my head bobbing between two choices. Again, the proverbial devil diva and angel sitting on my shoulders. On one side, a camoclad Bianca begged me to turn back and confess my love to Jack. But on the other shoulder, a designer-dressed career woman urged me to press on and not miss my flight. In the end, the career woman won. Her voice rang louder than the other woman. And no wonder, since I've spent much more time putting business over romance.

I fumble my fingers over the seatbelt once more, then drop it and sigh. The flight attendants step toward the front, and the captain's voice pours over the speakers. What have I done? Plenty of flights leave for Chicago every day. And I know of at least three men at the office who would gladly take my place at the bike shop. But Jack.

Would I ever get another chance to talk with Jack?

I spring to my feet and race toward the exit. A flight attendant in the back is closing the door to the plane. Her eyes widen as I nearly knock her over. "I'm so sorry, but I need out." She takes a step back as if she's happy to let the crazy woman off her flight. I cross onto the jetway as the door shuts behind me.

As I start back toward the airport, the bridge shifts. I cling to the side, staring out the glass panels. Seriously? I thought these things never moved. Especially in a place as busy as Atlanta. I tighten my grip and wait for it to stop. Once it parks again, I run inside the airport, not knowing what terminal I've entered. I crane my neck to read the signs.

My best bet is to call Jack. With any luck, he may still be in the parking lot. Or at least in Atlanta.

I pat my jacket pockets, then my jeans pockets, and wince. I left my phone in my purse and my purse on the plane. I hurry to the nearest window and watch a plane from my airline lift into the air.

The higher the plane flies, the farther my jaw drops. Trying not to panic, I speed toward the nearest desk.

"Hi." I smile nervously at the young man wearing a "Stephen" nametag.

"Yes, can I help you?" Stephen lifts his eyebrows as if asking me to get on with it.

"Yes, I left my purse on a plane that I'm pretty sure is on its way to Chicago."

He studies me with a blank stare. "Okay . . ."

"Flight 458 to Chicago."

"Might I ask how your purse got on the plane without you?"

"I was on the plane, but then I got off."

"I see." Stephen blinks, not the least bit of concern on his face. "And why would you do that?"

"Look, there was this guy. He came confessing his love for me, then I didn't know what to do, so I got on my flight, and—"

Stephen yawns wide enough to swallow a bowling ball.

"Did you just yawn?"

He shrugs. "What do you want me to do?"

I take a second to calm down before responding. "Can you call the flight and tell them to send my purse back? And the rest of my luggage?"

"Sure . . ." He backs up a few inches and slants his eyes as if I've scared him. And maybe I have. But the thought of not having Jack scares me. "I need your name and seat number."

I smile. "Bianca Manderson, seat 22A."

Stephen picks up the phone, and I swear he rolls his eyes. Nevertheless, he makes the call and thanks whomever is on the other end of the line, then hangs up. "There's another flight coming here from Chicago tonight. They will transfer your belongings to that flight."

I suck in a breath and nod. That will have to do. I have no other choice. "Thanks. Can I give them a number to call when it arrives?"

"They will call the number used to book your ticket."

"Ariel." I whisper to myself, then bite my lip. I look at

Stephen. "Thanks." I tap my hand on his desk and start toward the parking lot. I'll get in my car, go to the office, and sort out the issue about my purse and luggage with Ariel.

Halfway there, I stop and slap my forehead. How stupid can I be? I hold my stomach and groan. My keys are in my purse. Along with everything else.

Having no other option, I slink back toward Stephen. "Hi, again."

This time, Stephen definitely rolls his eyes. What's with this guy? People like him give airlines a bad name. To make matters worse, he now has people coming by to board the plane.

I move to the side so he can check tickets. "I need to borrow your phone, please."

He ignores me.

"Stephen, uh, Mr. Stephen, please?"

He continues to ignore me.

"I'm begging you."

He presses his lips together and flares his nostrils. I swear I see steam rise from them.

"Please, I'm begging you in the name of love."

He shakes his head. "Go to the back of this line and wait your turn."

I exaggerate a sigh. "Thanks." With the morning I'm having, what's a few extra minutes?

Hanging my head, I creep toward the back of the line, which now wraps all the way to the windows. I plant myself behind the last person and peer out the window impatiently.

Is that? I tilt my head for a better view. Something resembling a deer head stares back at me from across the airport. Not having much to lose with being the last in line, I walk closer to examine further. Sure enough, a deer. Moving backwards with the help of Jack . . . and some woman . . . with her arm around his shoulder.

I frown, and start to get back in line, then smile. Who cares? He can have ten women beside him, and I'd still want to go to him. I stand like statue for a moment, watching the trio grow smaller in view. What am I doing? If I run, I might catch them.

I dart away from the terminal, happy that the turquoise boots run better than any pair of heeled shoes I've ever purchased. I lose sight of them near some shops, then spot the deer again on a downward escalator. Assuming they're leaving, I make a beeline for the parking lot. Maybe I can head them off. The sun hits my face when I emerge from the glass doors. I shade my eyes, because of course my sunglasses are on their way to Chicago with the rest of my necessities. Deer horns glisten in the distance.

Time to put my cardio skills to use. I start sprinting ahead, eyes fully focused on the deer as more of it and Jack emerge. I can almost see their full figures when a loud honk blasts my right ear.

I freeze, my heart pounding. A van stops a few feet from me, the driver red-faced and spouting off words I'd never say aloud. I mouth a sorry and meander from the center of the parking lot to in between two rows of cars before I continue running.

It takes me a moment to spot Jack and the deer again. And the dark hair of a woman. I roll my eyes. But I'll deal with her after I get to Jack. I run a few more yards, only slowing down when my knee hits the fender of a Cadillac parked too close to the car in front of it.

I hold my knee as I stumble-run forward. At last, I'm within reach of Jack, the deer, and the mystery woman, who happens to have the same exact hairstyle as Ariel. Too out of breath to yell, I leap toward them and hug my arms around the deer.

When I do, it rolls back, pulling me to the ground. Jack stops and turns around, obviously feeling the tug.

"Bianca!" Pure joy spreads across his handsome face. He reaches down and lifts me to my feet. Exhausted and clumsy from the fall, I stumble. He wraps an arm behind me and lifts me up onto the back of the deer as if he were placing a kid on a carousel horse. He keeps one arm around me for support and brushes the stray hairs from my eyes.

"Ariel?" I blink, catching a front view of the mysterious woman for the first time.

She waves. "He came to the office looking for you. I helped him get here."

I grin, sending a silent "thank you" to my friend.

She smiles. "I'll give you two a minute."

I nod, then focus on Jack. I take a few deep breaths to bring my heartbeat back to semi-normal before I speak. "Jack, I'm sorry I didn't come sooner."

"No, it's okay. I know I burst in all of a sudden. And I anticipated that you might be mad about me selling the land after blowing up on you."

I drop my gaze and shake my head. As I raise my eyes to Jack, a tear trickles down my cheek. "No, it shocked me—confused me, too." I shrug. "But I'm happy for you."

His shoulders relax, and he smiles. "I meant every word I said in the airport. I've been miserable since you left."

"Me, too." I wipe a tear from my eye.

Jack catches my hand in his before I drop it from my face. "You too, what?"

"I've been miserable without you. And I realize it's because I love you."

The words barely leave my lips before Jack's mouth is on mine. He moves his hand from my face to cradle the back of my head and plunges his fingers into my tangled hair. I wrap my arms around his neck, content to be back in his embrace at last.

So many times I've replayed our first kiss, and all those that followed, including the last kiss that literally set things on fire. No kiss could've topped that one. Until this one.

After a few minutes, we pull apart, and I rest my forehead on his chest. I let out a long sigh, as if I've just received a medal for enduring a grueling triathlon.

Jack hugs me tighter. "Sorry you missed your flight."

I push back and frown. "Are you kidding? There's three men at the office begging to take this trip. Besides, there's no place I'd rather be than here with you . . ." I glance down. "Sitting on this deer."

We both laugh, and I hear Ariel cackle. I twist to see her holding up her phone.

"What are you doing?"

"Videoing this, of course. You'll thank me one day."

I roll my eyes before turning back to Jack.

"I don't have guests coming in until tomorrow. Would you like to show me around Atlanta?"

"You'll have to drive, since my license is in the air."

"Huh?" He slants his eyes toward the sky in confusion.

I giggle. "I left the plane in such a hurry, I forgot my purse under the seat. Along with my wallet, phone, keys, and sunglasses."

He grins. "You were that excited to see me, huh?"

My lips curve into a smile. "Always, Jack Jackson. And since I'm technically supposed to be on a business trip for three days, I'd love to spend those days in Alabama, checking out the new site for Macon and Ronald's upcoming store. After my belongings land, of course." I click my tongue. "That is, if I won't interfere with your work."

His grin grows into a smile so wide that it stretches across his entire face. "Are you kidding? I'd love nothing more than to have you spend time with me. Three couples are coming, so you'll make a nice hostess for the ladies. And I can't wait for them to meet the woman who bagged this buck."

I narrow my eyes. "Since when did you start referring to yourself as a buck?"

He laughs. "I was referring to this old boy." He lifts his hand from my waist and slaps the deer on the rear. When he does, it starts rolling down the slight incline of the parking lot.

"Whoa." I grip the horns and grit my teeth, hanging on for dear life. This may be it. I just might die by someone hitting a deer . . . in the Atlanta airport parking lot. Luckily, Jack catches up to me before any cars come too close. My heart flips over in my chest as I cling to his shirt.

"I got the whole thing." Ariel waves from a few yards back, holding her phone with the other hand.

I shake my head at Ariel, then stare down at the deer. "Are these bullet holes?"

"Yeah . . ." Jack palms the back of his neck with his free hand and blushes. "I'll explain that in a minute. But all you need to know now is how much I love you."

I lift my gaze to his gorgeous eyes and smile. I smooth a hand across his clean-shaven cheek and pull him in for a kiss.

No doubt, anyone passing by will balk at the couple making out in the parking lot, while the girl sits atop a stuffed deer on skates. But if they only knew Jack Jackson and how much I love him, they'd think nothing of it.

EPILOGUE

One Year Later

Bianca

I veer off the highway, following a path of balloons that line the end of the paved road leading to the new store. As my car winds through the drive, a huge metal building appears through the trees. The Outdoorsmen Oasis logo pops up as I top the hill.

My stomach swirls as I park my car around the back of the new store. I've gone to a few grand openings for Macon and Ronald's new franchises over the past year, but this one is special. It's on the back of Jack's hunting camp, and it represents, in a way, our relationship. If it weren't for working with this client, I'd never have met Jack. And if it weren't for this particular store, I'd have no reason to come back.

Well, except for Jack, of course.

A year ago, I rode off into the sunrise on a stuffed deer.

Since then, we've worn out the roads between Atlanta and Apple Cart, visiting one another whenever work allows. But that will soon change, and I can't wait to tell Jack.

I open my door and step onto the asphalt, the fresh tarry aroma itching my nostrils. Balloons of all earthy colors swirl around the front entrance. I push them aside, careful not to let one pop as I shut the door.

My eyes gravitate to the tall ceiling, then to the large display of stuffed and mounted animals on the back wall. Each of the Outdoorsmen Oasis stores displays an array of local wildlife as a focal point for their stores. The Alabama store includes deer, turkey, squirrels, hogs, and several smaller species of birds. Macon offered to put my deer between the busts of the deer he and Ronald shot at the lodge. And, although flattered, I declined his offer in favor of keeping it at Jack's place. Plus, it might put a damper on the decor as it has a broken antler and a lot of bullet holes.

Crazy as it sounds, that deer is also a symbol of my relationship with Jack. The deer itself is strong and can withstand a lot. Its bullet holes represent all the challenges it has faced. And the skates make it easier to transport, which fits with all our commuting these days.

Thank goodness, those days are coming to an end.

I slip in the door that leads to the back offices, where I told Jack to meet me before the opening. I find him sitting on the edge of a conference table, throwing darts at the wall. I knock on the side of the open door to avoid startling him.

He turns toward my knock. "Hey." He sets the dart he's holding on the table and makes it across the room in two huge steps. Then, he wraps his arms around my waist and picks me up, planting a huge kiss on my lips. I squeeze my arms around his neck for a tight hug before he returns my heels to the floor.

"It's nice out there, isn't it?" I nod back toward the front of the store.

"It's nicer in here with you." He winks, and my cheeks tingle. Even after a year, his winking still makes me blush. I hope that never changes.

"I've got news."

Jack drops one arm and leads me to the table with his other. "Let's hear it." He pulls out a chair and motions for me to sit, then sits on the edge of the table beside me.

"Dad is retiring in a few months."

"Yeah?" He narrows his eyes. Probably because this is old news. Dad announced his retirement just after the new year.

"So, he's offering some stake in the company to all of my half-sisters and me but making me the CEO."

"That's what we expected, right?"

"I'm getting to the cool part." I shift in my chair, excitement bubbling up in my throat. "I discussed things with Dad and my sisters, and everyone is fine with the office going remote."

"Cool, so when you're not traveling you get to work from your apartment in yoga pants all day?"

"Or from Alabama."

His mouth creeps into a huge smile. "What are you saying?"

I shrug. "I'm saying that eventually, I'll be open to maybe moving. You know, if it's for a good reason." I bat my eyes and smile.

He laughs. "Could you work in yoga pants if you moved here?"

I slap his wrist and roll my eyes. "What do you seriously think?"

He scratches his chin. "I think I need to give you my surprise a little early."

"Your surprise?"

"Yeah. Come on." He holds out a hand. I take it, and he pulls me to my feet. He leads me outside to his truck. I wrinkle my brow. What and where is this surprise?

He opens my door and motions for me to climb inside. I grip the handle above the window and pull myself into the seat. I have no idea where Jack plans on going, but we have less than an hour before Macon and Ronald cut the ribbon alongside the leaders of Apple Cart.

We turn onto the highway, then circle back toward the lodge entrance. A few minutes later, Jack opens my door to Chocolate and Brownie wagging toward us from his front porch. I get out and pet the dogs.

"Give me a sec." Jack runs up the front steps and inside. I stand in the middle of the yard, clueless.

A minute later, he returns with a something in his hand. As he comes closer, my lips tug into a smile. "Is that . . .?"

"Yep, Paul helped me locate more fish mitts." He lifts the ugly oven mitt with its mouth facing downward.

"That's my surprise?" Seriously, I don't see the urgency in this.

He nods. "Here, try it on."

He lowers the mitt and holds it flat on his palm for me to wear. I slide my hand inside and twist my lips. Something hits my fingertips. Something solid. I slide my thumb into the top part as well to grip the object and pull it out.

A ring. A beautiful diamond ring. I stare at it glistening in the sun, and my throat clogs. My hand tingles as I set it in my palm and examine it. For all I know, some poor woman lost her ring in a fish mitt before selling it to Paul. When I finally lift my eyes from the ring, Jack is on one knee in front of me, holding his cap in his hand.

Was he . . .? Was this . . .? My mouth drops as he nods, answering my silent inquiries.

"Bianca Claire Manderson, will you marry me?"

Jack's face blurs as my eyes start to water. I nod vigorously, still unable to find my voice. I leap forward into his arms, hugging him tightly. He laughs as the dogs come over to congratulate us by wagging their tails and nudging us with their noses.

I blink the tears from my eyes and pull back to look at my fiancé. I drop my arm from his neck and uncurl my hand to view the ring. "This is gorgeous. How long have you had it?"

He takes it from my hand and slides it onto my left ring finger. "A month or so. I decided that no matter where we live, I want to be with you. We just needed to figure out some logistics first."

"And then I mentioned possibly moving here."

He smiles. "Yes, you did."

"I never thought I'd say this, but I think country living is starting to grow on me."

He smiles wider. "I will gladly let you name and feed all baby animals, as well as stock one of the hall closets completely with scentless makeup."

I giggle and lay my head on his chest. "Sounds like a great life to me."

"Great life indeed," he whispers against my ear, then kisses my forehead.

I glance at my ring, understanding why Ariel gawks at hers all the time. It is more than just a gorgeous diamond. It is a symbol of having someone who loves me unconditionally and more than I could imagine. I gaze up at Jack's handsome face and the lines of trees filling the background behind us. An even better view than my ring.

Yeah, we will definitely make our life in Apple Cart.

🦌🦌

If you enjoyed *Hunting for Love*, you'll enjoy reading all about Tanner finding his HEA in *Chicken about Love*. I'd also love it if you left a review to help other readers find my books.

ACKNOWLEDGMENTS

First, I would like to thank God for giving me creative ideas and placing the right people in my path to help see them to fruition.

My husband, Blake, gets credit next for always supporting my writing endeavors, even if he finds my stories a little too "girly and Hallmarkish." But this one wasn't too bad.

I also want to thank Matthew Rushing with Wilderness Whitetails Alabama for answering all my unusual questions and giving me first-hand insight into the world of managing a hunting lodge. Many of the personal touches, such as serving deer poppers and grilled honeybuns as well as recording the hunts, came straight from Matthew's own experience. If you're ever in the "hunt" for great deer hunting accommodations, check them out in Fayette, Alabama. Find them online and on Facebook.

ABOUT THE AUTHOR

Kaci Lane is a journalist turned fiction writer who believes all stories should have a happy ending. While unsuccessfully trying to learn Spanish for a decade, she has become fluent in sarcasm, Southern belle and movie quotes. She is married to a Southern Gentleman and has two young children who help keep her humility in check. Connect with her on kacilane.com or follow her on Amazon for upcoming releases.

P.S.

You might be a redneck family if you hit a deer with your car, then call your husband to tell him what ditch it landed in so that he can get it for the meat. (True story!)

BOOKS BY KACI LANE

Schooled on Love Series

Taco Truck Takedown

Side Hustle

Buggy List

Off-Season

No Brides Club Series

No Time for Traditions

Bama Boys Series

Hunting for Love

Chicken about Love

Hammered by Love

Bama Boys related stand alone:

Christmas in Dixie

*If you enjoyed *Hunting for Love*, you will enjoy *Christmas in Dixie*, which features some of the same characters during the holiday season in Apple Cart County.